The Scorpion

By James A. Anderson

THE SCORPION

Copyright 2012 by James A. Anderson

All Rights Reserved. Except for brief excerpts for review purposes, no part of this publication may be reproduced, distributed or transmitted in any form or by any means, or stored on a database or retrieval system, without the written permission of the author or publisher.

The characters, places and events in this book are fictitious or used in a fictitious way. Any similarity to real persons, either living or dead, is coincidental and not intended by the author.

Published by CreateSpace
Cover Design by CreateSpace
Printed in the United States of America

ISBN(10) – 1470109689
ISBN (13) – 978-1470109684

Books by James A. Anderson

The Scorpion (2012)

Deadline (2010)

Author's Note

This is my second novel and there are many people to thank in its preparation. My thanks and great appreciation to those family members and friends who read the early drafts and offered useful comments and suggestions to improve the manuscript: Sherry Anderson, Joan Anderson, Peter Anderson, Lawrence Otis, Terry Otis, and my daughter Amanda and her husband Jeff. Any errors or omissions are entirely the author's.

A special thanks to my wife, best friend and soul mate, Sherry, for her love, understanding and patience during the writing process.

JAMES A. ANDERSON

For Mike and Amanda,

Our children

The value of marriage is not that adults produce children but that children produce adults -- Peter De Vries (1910-1993)

THE SCORPION

JAMES A. ANDERSON

DAY ONE

SUNDAY

THE SCORPION

PROLOGUE

SANAA, YEMEN

My father hath chastised you with whips, but I will chastise you with scorpions. - I Kings ch. 12, v. 11

THE SCORPION

THE STING of the scorpion brings agonizing death.

A scorpion crawled along the sand. The deadly arachnid inched its way on the ground on its eight legs, with two lobster-like pincers searching for something to grab. The venomous stinger coiled in its tail ready to launch.

It crawled close to a group of men standing around a long metal table in the large white-canopied tent in the desert on the outskirts of the city. It edged towards a leg – a possible target for its deadly sting.

Suddenly a foot crashed down, crushing its shell and sending the arachnid into oblivion.

"Too bad little fella, there is room for only one scorpion in this room," laughed the owner of the leg. The others around the table joined in the merriment.

The man was six-foot, two inches in height and weighed about 190 pounds. Abdul al-Sharif was his birth name. But in many corners of the world he was more commonly known as The Scorpion.

He was a faceless, nameless terrorist whose deadly sting was felt in many forms of destruction – bombs, assassination and poison. He did whatever was necessary to achieve his aims and the objectives of his Al-Qaeda faction.

"Let us get back to the important business at hand," said the heavily bearded man at the head of the long metal table.

His name was Sheikh Saif al-Islam, head of the Al-Qaeda cell in Yemen. He wore a long red caftan with black stripes. His face was leathery with a large scar running down his left cheek, remnants from an old shrapnel wound picked up while serving in Afghanistan with his leader Osama bin Laden.

Until recently, bin Laden was hiding out in Pakistan, but dispatched al-Islam to head the terrorist faction working out of Yemen, a loyal supporter of the Islamic jihad. Then his exalted leader was killed by the accursed Americans in a Navy Seals operation that attacked bin Laden's compound in Abbotabad, just 61 kilometers north of Islamabad, Pakistan's capital.

"Yes, the plans for our newest operation against the Western infidels are ready to launch," stated Abdul Rahman, al-Islam's lieutenant who stood next to him. "This will strike a telling blow that will make the World Trade Towers seem like an incidental side show. It will strike fear into the hearts of the Godless Americans and their allies. It will show how we can bring the wrath of Allah on to the heads of those who would support the United States. We will accomplish this by attacking its closest neighbor and ally – Canada. Security is weak there and they are ripe for the taking."

He walked over to a nearby easel with photos and diagrams of their targets and outlined details of the operation.

Rahman turned to al-Sharif. "Brother al-Sharif, are you ready to begin your journey to head up our forces to strike this telling blow for Islam?"

THE SCORPION

The Scorpion bowed his head. "I am. Allah truly will be with us in the success of this operation."

Sheikh al-Islam put his hands forward to the gathering of the six men. "Allah is with you all, my brothers. May the sting of the Scorpion strike at the heart of our enemies!"

The group dispersed. The Scorpion eyed one person leaving by a side entrance. It was Ashraf Douad, one of the junior lieutenants. The slim, young man slinked out of the tent alone and wandered down the dusty trail. The Scorpion followed silently from a distance.

He saw Douad enter an alleyway. He shadowed him.

Douad leaned against a wall and pulled a cell phone from the folds of his caftan. He then texted a message.

The Scorpion smiled and confronted him.

He held a knife with a curved six-inch blade. He stared into the frightened brown eyes of the man and suddenly plunged the blade into the target's abdomen. He twisted the knife sharply with a sudden jerk. Douad clutched at his stomach as his pink intestines spilled out.

"Die like the gutted traitorous pig you are!" said the Scorpion who grasped the cell phone and checked the text message that was sent:

TARGET CANADA.

THE SCORPION.

OPERATION SALADIN PREPARED TO LAUNCH.

CHAPTER 1

LONDON, ENGLAND

TREVOR TREVANIAN worked furiously at the keyboard of his Mac Powerbook laptop.

The book was going well. He was two-thirds of the way through it. His contract with McLelland and Stewart Publishers in Toronto called for the book to be delivered by August 1 so it could be released in their fall line-up.

Trevanian, the foreign correspondent for the Toronto Daily Express, had been in Afghanistan and in August of 2010 was kidnapped by Al-Qaeda and spirited away to Pakistan where he met and interviewed Osama bin Laden. (See DEADLINE by James A. Anderson, published by Lulu.com, 2010).

The story was a worldwide sensation, which made Trevanian a household name and launched the struggling Daily Express into the pantheon of great newspapers such as the Washington Post and New York Times. The paper had been sitting fourth in circulation out of the five Toronto newspapers. It was now in second place just behind the Toronto Star and much healthier financially.

Two months after the incident, Trevanian was transferred by the newspaper to London as the paper's European correspondent. While he missed the excitement of the Afghanistan post, Trevanian relished the prestige of the European assignment. It was also much less hazardous to his health. He was not as likely to get shot or blown up.

His newfound celebrity in the news media also brought his book contract. He wrote about his kidnapping and the experiences of interviewing bin Laden, followed by the adventure and difficulties in filing his story. London was a great place to work on his book and the pubs were fabulous.

Trevanian glanced at his watch. 12:15 pm. Pangs of hunger were starting to surface. He decided it was time to break for lunch.

Trevanian left his apartment and headed down the street to his favorite hangout, the Elephant and Castle. He slid into a booth and was greeted by Cathy, a waitress who regularly served him.

"Hello, luv! What'll it be today?" Cathy handed him a menu, but Trevanian only glanced at it. He was familiar with their fare – traditional British pub grub. "I fancy your Steak and Kidney pie with mashed potatoes, Cathy. And darlin' bring me a pint of Tennant's lager."

"Anything that suits your fancy, Trev. Coming right up."

"So how are those two flat coats of yours doing these days?"

"Fine, luv. They are good company. More reliable than most men." Cathy was a dog lover and had two flat coat retrievers Derry and Navarre. "I'll be right

THE SCORPION

back with your drink."

As Trevanian sat waiting, he glanced around the pub, which was jammed full as usual with the lunchtime crowd. A tall, heavy-set man sitting at the bar was watching him in return. He picked up his drink and wandered over to Trevanian. He sat down opposite and placed his beer on the table. The man looked to be in his forties, partly balding and wore large black rimmed glasses – regular nerd ware.

"Mr. Trevanian, you don't know me, but we are well aware of you and your reputation. I take it you are enjoying London. Must be a little sedate after your experiences in Afghanistan and Pakistan," said the man.

"Yes, but it's a welcome change. And you are?"

"The name is Wilton, Charles Wilton."

"Well, Mr. Wilton nice to meet you, but I'm just catching a bit of lunch. Is there something I can do for you?"

"There is actually. I work for a government service and we have a great interest in your work. My boss would like to have a word with you."

"And who would that be? The police or perhaps MI-5?" Trevanian thought the man looked like a cop or more likely a British spook. He was tall and heavy-set with a weasel-like face and beady eyes.

"Not far wrong. Let's just say I am in the Foreign Service."

"Aaah! Then you're MI-6."

Cathy arrived back with Trevanian's drink. "Your food will be up in a minute, Trev."

She addressed Wilton: "Anything for you, sir?"

"No thanks, luv. I am just fine with what I have."

Wilton turned back to Trevanian. "I'd rather not get into specifics here, Mr. Trevanian. May I call you Trevor?"

"Sure. All my friends do. And what can I do for you gentlemen in the Foreign Service? Do you have a good story for me?"

Wilton looked back at Trevanian with horror on his face. "My God, certainly not. We really don't like being in the press."

"Then what can I do for you?"

"We would like to talk with you on a highly confidential basis. I will wait over at the bar while you enjoy your lunch, Trevor. But I would ask you to accompany me to our headquarters for a little chat." With that, Wilton arose and returned to his bar stool.

Just then Cathy came back with Trevor's food. He tucked in heartily, thinking: *Well, at least they are not spiriting me away with a hood over my head!*

* * *

Since he had been in England, Trevor never could get used to driving on the wrong side of the road. The English drove on the left and everything was reversed to what most of the rest of the world did. Trust the Brits! That is why Trevor never drove over here. Instead, he used taxis and the Underground or the Tube as it is better known here.

He sat quietly in the front seat of Charles Wilton's Vauxhall during the drive through the streets of London. Trevor gazed out the window as they passed by Buckingham Palace, Whitehall and through Trafalgar Square with Lord Nelson standing proudly atop his column.

Within minutes, they were in southwestern London on the bank of the River Thames. They entered Vauxhall Cross. The Babylon-on-Thames or Legoland was just ahead. That is the Security Intelligence Service or MI-6 Building. Its resemblance to an ancient Babylonian Ziggurat gave rise to the nicknames.

The MI-6 Building was approved by former British Prime Minister Margaret Thatcher and it has appeared in *The Tailor of Panama* and a number of James Bond films, including *GoldenEye, The World Is Not Enough* and *Die Another Day*. On September 20, 2000, the building was attacked with a rocket, which only caused some superficial damage.

The Vauxhall entered an underground garage and Wilton flashed his ID at the security post guarding the entrance to the Babylon-on-Thames.

Within 15 minutes, Trevor found himself in the office of the Assistant Director of MI-6. *Guess I'm not important enough to meet M, the big boss, herself.*

Hugh Pettigrew, the Assistant Director, introduced himself to Trevanian and offered him a seat on a couch near a glass coffee table in his office. Pettigrew sat opposite Trevanian.

"So, what have I done to bring attention to myself from Britain's top spook shop?" quipped Trevanian, feeling slightly uncomfortable. Intelligence services had that effect on him, especially since his run-in with the Pakistani ISI last year.

Pettigrew just smiled. "Oh my dear chap, nothing to worry about. We just wanted to have a little chat with you. Are you enjoying your stay in Britain? A lot more civilized than your previous posting, I dare say."

"Oh, I don't know. Afghanistan's not too bad if you don't mind dodging IEDs (Improvised Explosive Devices) and Islamic terrorists."

"Quite," said Pettigrew. "I must say we are quite impressed at your journalistic coup to snag an interview with Osama bin Laden. You must have quite the network of contacts with Al-Qaeda. The Americans finally took care of that son of a bitch – may he roast in hell. But we would dearly love to get our hands on the rest of his shady flock. I don't suppose you could share any information where we could begin to look for his lieutenants and his successor, that motherfucker Ayman al-Zawahiri.

"Sorry, I can't help you out with that. I was kidnapped by Al-Qaeda and taken to Pakistan, somewhere in the tribal areas of northern Pakistan. I have no idea where, since they had me wearing a hood most of the time. But even if I did know, I'm not sure I would pass that information on to you. Not my job, my dear chap. You know, journalistic integrity and all that."

"Right. Well, Mr. Trevanian as an Intelligence Agency we gather our information on our enemies in many different ways. You may not be aware, but we do have a number of journalists on our payroll who do provide some useful information from time to time. You news people often have access to people and things that can be helpful in the fight to preserve our security. You can't really support the objectives of these terrorists, surely."

"Of course not, and I would never do or sanction anything to harm my country or innocent people,' replied Trevanian. "But as journalists, we try not to choose sides. We just report the news. It is up to our readers to make up their own minds about who is right or wrong. There are two sides to every story and sometimes three or four. Not everything is black and white."

"Yes, but these people are criminals and animals who blow up innocent people in their cause," Pettigrew protested.

"Someone once observed that one person's terrorist is another person's freedom fighter. You Brits used to call the Israelis terrorists and some of those 'terrorists' ended up running the country, even becoming Prime Minister. I'm sure even George Washington was considered a terrorist or traitor in his day by your government. If you'd won the Revolutionary War, he likely would have been hanged. It's the winners who write history. So times and situations change, Mr. Pettigrew. I don't need a lecture on patriotism, thank you very much."

"So I suppose you wouldn't be interested in joining our little network of correspondents, Mr. Trevanian. We pay quite handsomely for useful information."

"I am afraid not, Mr. Pettigrew. I've never wanted to be a spy. Although I do love the James Bond films."

"They're not really a realistic picture of what we do. I am afraid Ian Fleming's imagination got the better of him and the film producers are not much better. John Le Carré's stuff is more like it. He was a former British intelligence man and certainly knows the trade."

"Well, I'm not interested in becoming a spook, Mr. Pettigrew. I am writing a book about my experiences in Afghanistan and Pakistan and my meeting with bin Laden. I suggest you read it when it comes out. I'll be happy to send you an autographed copy."

"Thank you, Mr. Trevanian. I think our business has ended. Sorry we couldn't come to an agreement. Charles will drive you home," said Pettigrew as he ushered Trevanian out the door.

After Trevanian left, Pettigrew moved to his desk. He picked up the phone and made a transatlantic call.

"Well, what did he have to say?" said the American voice on the other end.

"Nothing useful," replied Pettigrew. "He turned down our offer to be an asset."

"That's too bad. The man has many contacts, especially with Al-Qaeda. He still could be of use to us. Keep a close eye on him."

Pettigrew ended the call. "Oh, you can be sure we will!"

CHAPTER 2

CIA HEADQUARTERS, LANGLEY, VIRGINIA

JAMES KNIGHT, Deputy Director of Operations for the Central Intelligence Agency, stared out the window of his upper floor office.

He viewed the rolling, green Virginia countryside and in the distance the city of Washington, D.C. with its many monuments and buildings. Knight could see in the distance the Washington monument and the Capitol Dome, symbols of the democracy he spent his life defending.

He turned back to face Barry Stovin, his chief of operations. "Our friends at MI-6 met with that Canadian journalist Trevor Trevanian. Unfortunately, he won't play ball. That's too bad. We were hoping he could provide some leads on the whereabouts of bin Laden's senior people. It would be a coup for us if we could nail those sons of bitches. I'm sure the President would be most grateful."

"Well sir, I am afraid that something big is afoot. We have word that a new operation is being launched. It comes from an agent highly placed in the Al-Qaeda hierarchy in Yemen."

"Do we know the target, Barry? Is it in the U.S.?"

"I am afraid we don't know much, sir. Apparently the target is in Canada.

Something called Operation Saladin. It is being headed by the Scorpion."

Knight's brow furrowed with deep concern. "Don't tell me that bastard has surfaced again. He is another Al-Qaeda son of a bitch I'd like to nail. We don't even know what he looks like. No one has any photos, fingerprints or anything. He works like a ghost and doesn't leave anyone alive to tell tales. Do we know what the target is in Canada and why there?"

"I am afraid not, sir," replied Stovin. "Our agent was only able to get out the basic information. I'm afraid he was discovered and killed. His body was found in Sanaa, Yemen – disemboweled and beheaded. Our analysts believe Canada was selected as a message to us and our allies."

"Poor sod!" muttered Knight. "Well, I need to give a heads up to our Canadian colleagues in CSIS. We had better put them on alert and offer any resources they need."

As Stovin left the office, Knight's phone rang. It was his private line. "Knight here," he answered.

"Darling, I just wanted to remind you that we have tickets tonight to the symphony at the Kennedy Centre." The voice belonged to his wife Diana. She was a cultural maven on the Washington scene, heavily involved in the arts community and high society.

Blast, just what I need. Another night of listening to bloody Beethoven or

Brahms, thought Knight.

"Listen, dear. I'm not sure I can make it tonight. We have a breaking situation here I have to deal with."

"You are not the only person in the CIA, James. I'm sure there are plenty of people to deal with any 'situation' as you call it. We have had these tickets for a month now and this program is the highlight of the symphony season. Yo Yo Ma is a guest performer. I'm on the symphony's board of directors and we are expected to attend these events. I want your ass in a seat next to mine if you know what's good for you. The concert is at 8 p.m." Diana's tone had a biting edge that would send chills down even a terrorist's spine.

"Yes, dear," replied Knight meekly. He learned long ago those two simple words were the secret to a happy marriage.

Knight started to punch in the numbers to call Ottawa and his counterpart in the Canadian Security Intelligence Service. He needed to inform the Canadians that the Scorpion was about to sting.

CHAPTER 3

TORONTO, CANADA

SUNDAY MORNING was a sunny, bright June day in Toronto. The view from Andrew Chase's luxury condo apartment on Lakeshore Drive offered a stunning sight of Lake Ontario, with its panorama of small yachts dotting the water and people strolling along the harbor.

Katie Cannon held her coffee as she gazed at the view. Katie was excited. Her wedding day was only a week away. And although many of the plans were set, there was still plenty to do. She wanted everything to be perfect.

She was marrying the man of her dreams -- Andrew Chase, the multimillionaire owner and publisher of the Toronto Daily Express, the newspaper where Katie worked as a reporter.

The wedding was set for Saturday, June 23 at St. Matthew's United Church. The dinner and reception were going to be held high atop Toronto in the revolving 360 restaurant in the CN Tower. It would be a gala social event of the year in the city with almost 300 invited guests, family, friends, and luminaries from the Toronto financial and publishing communities.

Katie had fond memories of the night Andrew proposed to her at dinner in that very restaurant. Along with her crème brûlée, came a 6-carot diamond ring and Andrew's proposal. Katie accepted without question.

"Hey honey, what's on tap today?" inquired Andrew coming out of the bathroom. He had showered, shaved and was ready to enjoy his Sunday after some breakfast.

"Well sweetie, we need to go over to the 360 Resturant at the tower first to finalize the menu," replied Katie. "Later this afternoon I have to go for my final dress fitting and you need to pick up your tux."

"Great. I'll go with you. I'm dying to see your dress!"

"No, no, no...that's verboten, Andrew. It's bad luck to see me in my dress before the wedding. You have to wait until I come down the aisle. You can go get your tux while I'm doing the fitting."

"What superstitious nonsense! You don't really believe that clap-trap , do you, Katie?"

"It's tradition, Andrew. And I don't want to take any chances. Besides, I want it to be a surprise."

"If you say so, hon. You usually get your way anyhow."

"That's right. And you better get used to it after we get married, buster!" Katie gave him a playful poke in the ribs.

Andrew just laughed. "Well, it's such a nice day. Perhaps later we could take a walk along the waterfront and have dinner at Captain Jack's." Captain Jack's was a floating seafood restaurant on a boat moored in the harbor and one of Katie and Andrew's favorite haunts.

Andrew gently took Katie by the arm and pulled her in close to him. His lips met hers. "Have I told you today how much I love you?"

"No, but feel free to express yourself as much as you want. I love you too, Andrew and I want this wedding to be the happiest day of our lives. I want it to be something we will always remember."

"I'm sure it will be, darling. I'm sure it will be."

* * *

Across town in his Bloor Street apartment, Braden Young was just finishing his breakfast and wondering what he would do today. It was a rare day off for him from the Daily Express.

Young was the paper's managing editor. He was a 57-year-old American journalist and editor hired by Andrew Chase two years ago to turn the paper around and boost its flagging circulation. And turn it around he had. The newspaper was now #2 in the Toronto market in circulation and advertising revenue was booming. The paper was financially healthy after a period where its future seemed in doubt.

But the job was all consuming. It left little time for a social life. Young's career led to the disintegration of his marriage with his wife Nancy and a divorce. He had been estranged from his only daughter Megan until last August when they were reunited during her own personal crisis.

Megan lived with him for a couple of months until she got her own life back on track. She found a job in Toronto and eventually got her own apartment. Braden got together with Megan weekly for dinner or brunch.

She had been all he had for a social life until a couple of months ago. Then he met Leah McCall, a Registered Nurse. They dated a few times as their busy schedules allowed and found they enjoyed each other's company. Braden was taking things slowly and that was fine with Leah who had been the victim of a previous abusive relationship. She found it hard to trust men, but she found Braden to be a decent, hard working guy and enjoyed his company.

Maybe I'll give Leah a call. If she's not working today perhaps we could do something. Perhaps go to a movie and dinner.

Braden picked up the phone.

CHAPTER 4

FRANKFURT INTERNATIONAL AIRPORT

THE TRANSIT LOUNGE was a busy place. It was jammed with travelers awaiting their connecting flights.

The Scorpion was among them. He had been aboard a flight from Yemen and now was waiting for his American Airlines flight to Logan International in Boston. The flight was scheduled to depart at 10:45 p.m. and arrive early Monday morning in Boston.

He would meet his team there. A squad of agents already was in place. They had infiltrated the infidel society of the Great Satan, just waiting for their call to duty and to Paradise.

They did not know the targets yet. The Scorpion would brief them on his arrival. They would be driving to Canada where it was easier to cross the border. Al-Qaeda had done its homework and knew the weak points of the border crossing. After all, with the longest border in the world, almost 5,000 miles of it, keeping it completely secure was impossible.

The Scorpion smiled at the thought of his mission. He would be bringing death and destruction to the infidels on a scale previously unheard of in North

America.

He fingered his British passport in the name of an alias, one of three he kept on his person. All three were very authentic looking and official. They would gain him entry anywhere in the world without question.

A voice came over the airport intercom announcing boarding for Flight 1225 to Boston, Massachusetts.

The Scorpion picked up his small black carry on bag and headed to the aircraft.

His mission was about to begin.

THE SCORPION

DAY TWO
MONDAY

CHAPTER 5

LOGAN INTERNATIONAL AIRPORT, BOSTON

THE 747 touched down on the runway and taxied into the terminal gate. It had been an uneventful flight.

The Scorpion had flirted with the pretty air steward. Her name was Sharlene and she was a blonde bombshell. Sharlene had a petite build, with close-cropped hair, azure blue eyes and large perky breasts.

She was the perfect picture of one of the virgins he could look forward to in Paradise when he arrived. That is if he really believed in such nonsense. But he didn't. He would leave that to the fools who sacrificed themselves for Allah. The Scorpion wasn't particularly religious. The Koran was just a tool – a means to an end. Revenge.

The Scorpion always had a way with women. He could be charming, debonair with a boyishly handsome face. He was tall, lean, with a wiry muscular build and a Middle Eastern tan that was not too dark. He was not really Arab looking at all. That was a plus when he went through security because they did not target him with close scrutiny in the usual profiling officials used to check for terrorists. And as far as he knew, there were no photos or fingerprints of him in any databases in the world.

The Scorpion was a faceless, nameless entity known only by reputation as a deadly killer and terrorist. Most of the people who crossed his path were dead. He made sure of that.

Anyway, sitting in first class he received extra attention from Sharlene, along with her phone number slipped to him on a napkin with a Scotch and soda. Too bad he would not be able to take her up on her offer. He would have enjoyed that. But there was no time for such pleasurable diversions. He had a mission to complete.

As he exited the aircraft with a friendly, longing smile from Sharlene, the Scorpion joined the throng of people moving through the terminal toward Customs and Immigration.

His eyes scanned the several queues at Customs posts. He was searching for a female officer. His charms worked much better on them and usually they gave him no hassle.

He spotted one. She was a black woman, rather heavy-set and plain looking with a bored expression on her face. The queue was also shorter in her line. He quickly moved into place.

She proved to be no problem. After chatting with him for a few minutes, she stamped his passport. As he moved toward the luggage carousels, he noticed she

THE SCORPION

wore a smile on her face. He had made her day. *Women are such vain fools.*

The Scorpion picked up his bag and entered the main arrivals area of the terminal. There were a number of people holding signs for arriving passengers. There, in the centre of the throng, was the one for him with the correct code word: Saladin.

"Allah Akbar (God is Great)," said the Scorpion to the young man wearing jeans and a red, checked short-sleeved shirt.

"And so is his sting," replied the man with the correct counter response. The two men wordlessly exited the terminal and walked to the parking garage where a Dodge Caravan awaited them.

"The others are waiting," said the driver who introduced himself as Hashim Hadi.

"Then let's not keep them waiting," replied the Scorpion. "We have Allah's work to do."

CHAPTER 6
TORONTO DAILY EXPRESS

THE NEWSROOM was a hive of activity. People scurried about, Tim Hortons coffee cups in hand. The early morning is a busy time as reporters prepare to go out on their assigned stories and copy editors are busy editing stories on their computer screens.

Managing Editor Braden Young was in his office busy checking his e-mail. Over 200 had accumulated during his weekend off, but many could be immediately discarded as junk or non-essential. Several contained story tips, which he saved for later action.

Paul O'Connor, the Daily Express's assistant managing editor, entered Young's office. "Morning, boss. Did you have a rough night? You look like shit."

"Thanks, Paul. It's nice to see you too. I've got a bit of a hangover, I'm afraid. Leah and I did dinner and a movie and then hit some of the clubs on Yonge Street. I'm afraid I overdid it. I'm getting too old for this clubbing and boozing."

"It's time you got married and settled down, old man. Leah sounds like a nice woman and you could do worse than marry a nurse to take care of you in your old age."

Braden just smiled. "As if. That view of nurses showing empathy is a crock. She just tells me 'You've got two feet and a heartbeat; get it yourself!' So what's up today, anything big?"

O'Connor checked the sheet he was carrying. "Well there are several interesting stories afoot. We've got that murder trial where that insurance CEO's wife is charged with shooting him with his own service pistol after an argument at their family dinner last Christmas Eve. He had been screwing his secretary. She has that high priced lawyer Clayton Evans defending her. I'm sure he'll be arguing temporary insanity."

"That trial should make for juicy reading. Who is covering the trial?" inquired Young.

"Donna Marie Pierce. Then we've got a man hit by a subway train yesterday at the Dundas Street station. Apparently he dropped a bag over the edge of the platform and was bent over trying to retrieve it when an oncoming train brushed him. Fortunately he didn't sustain life threatening injuries – only a broken arm and some major body abrasions."

"He's one lucky guy. Those trains move pretty fast. He could have been swept right off that platform. Have whoever is on the story do a sidebar on transit safety and the dos and don'ts of subway travel."

O'Connor glanced back at his sheet. "And our Ottawa correspondent Bob

Wyatt has a follow up story on the controversy over the government's pending deal to spend $9 billion on the purchase of the F35 stealth fighter jet for the armed forces. The opposition Liberals are putting the government under fire and threatening to cancel the deal if they take power."

"All good grist for the mill," replied Young. "It sounds like a promising line-up, Paul. I need you to send in Katie Cannon to talk to me. I have a tip on a good story shaping up at St. Luke's Hospital. Apparently there is a three-year-old girl, Emily Carter, in a coma with a degenerative neurological disorder. The doctors say there is no hope for recovery – she's brain dead and in a vegetative state. They want to remove the breathing tube and give the child palliative care to die.

The parents are opposed and have hired a lawyer to fight the hospital's decision. The hospital has applied to the Consent and Capacity board for permission to remove life support. I think this story has far reaching implications for the ethical debate on who decides when we die and parental rights. But it is a touchy and sensitive story and I think Katie is the right person to handle it."

"Right, I'll send her in, Braden." O'Connor turned and left the office, back into the newsroom hive.

It was shaping up into another busy day for the Toronto Daily Express.

CHAPTER 7

LONDON, ENGLAND

TREVOR TREVANIAN spent the morning working on his book. Things were moving along swiftly.

The previous night he worked late filing a story to the Toronto Daily Express on Britain's problems in delivering adequate home care for the elderly. It was a story Canadians could empathize with since they too were facing a crisis in dealing with an aging population.

The story highlighted the need for more money to be pumped into home care for the elderly because of the shortage of long-term care facilities. Trevor personalized the story by highlighting the case of David Davenport who was struggling to care for his wife Lou, a victim of Pick's Disease, a form of dementia. Lou could not be left unattended and David quit his job as a construction worker to provide full-time home care to his wife. She needed help dressing, eating, bathing and coping with all the daily basic functions of life.

The British government provided some personal support workers for six hours throughout the week to help with bathing and house cleaning and to give Davenport a needed break from his duties. But he had been fighting with the social affairs ministry for more support and some money to help with mounting expenses.

Trevor's article argued the need for more funding for home care support to deal with a growing problem as the baby boomer population aged.

"As the population ages, there is no way we are going to be able to fund enough long-term care beds," he wrote. "The only way we can handle it is through home-care situations."

Trevor glanced at his watch. Almost lunch time. He closed up his laptop and headed out the door.

As he continued along the sidewalk to the nearby Elephant and Castle, a pert, young brunette, walked towards him carrying a small attaché case. She was thirtyish, very attractive, with a fine-boned face and sculpted chin. As she neared Trevor, she suddenly stumbled on the pavement and fell forward, her attaché case slipping to the ground. Trevor instinctively reached out to catch her, pulling her tightly in against his body.

"Shit! These damn heels will be the death of me yet," she cursed.

"Nice to meet you," Trevor smiled. "Are you OK? You took quite a stumble there. Maybe you should ditch those high heels."

"Wish I could, but I only wear them for work. I hope I didn't break them." Trevor let go and she steadied herself, lifting her left leg to check her heel.

"Hi there, my name is Trevor," he said. "What's your name and what do you do for a living?"

"Oh, I'm a reporter for the Daily Telegraph. My name is Lynne. Lynne Whitfield. I was just on my way back to Fleet Street after an interview. It was such a nice day I thought I would walk instead of taking the Tube. Bad idea, I guess."

"I don't know about that Lynne. Otherwise we might never have met. I'm a journalist also. A foreigner stationed here. I write for the Toronto Daily Express. Trevor Trevanian."

"Trevanian. My God, you're that Canadian bloke who met Osama bin Laden!"

"One and the same. And my head is still attached to my shoulders."

"I would give my first born for a story like that. You made headlines around the world."

"Yeah, it did stir up a little bit of a fuss," said Trevanian modestly.

"I'd love to hear more about that meeting and your interview." Lynne gazed at Trevor hopefully. Her green eyes twinkled with anticipation and she smiled warmly back at him. She hoped she wasn't being too brazen. But Lynne was not averse to bold moves to get what she wanted. "Perhaps we could get together for a drink sometime."

"Well actually, Lynne, I was about to grab some lunch at this pub down the street. How about joining me?"

"Love to. But it will be my treat, Trevor. Consider it a reward for being my knight in shining armor and rescuing a damsel in distress."

"Somehow I doubt you're a damsel who needs rescuing." Trevor placed his hand lightly on her back and ushered her down the street to the Elephant and Castle.

As they sat down in a booth near the front window, Cathy came over with menus. Trevor ordered a lager, while Lynne just opted for mineral water.

"Excuse me a moment, Trevor. I need to use the powder room. You just go ahead and order for me. You probably know this place well so I'll go with whatever you recommend."

Lynne arose and headed to the back of the pub where the Lads and Lassies rooms were located.

Cathy returned soon after Lynne departed. "So Trevor, who is the bird? She your girlfriend?"

Trevor thought he detected a note of hostility in Cathy's tone. "No, Cathy. It's just a business lunch. She is a fellow journalist. We're just comparing notes."

"Right," said Cathy with a hint of envy. "What'll it be today?"

"I think we'll just have the Welsh rarebit. Make sure the cheese is nice and bubbly."

"Two Welsh rarebits with bubbly cheese coming right up," replied Cathy, hustling off to the kitchen.

After Lynne entered the Lassies toilet, she pulled out her mobile and made a call.

"This is Gemini. Contact made with the target."

The voice on the other end said: "Good. Get better acquainted and stay close to him!"

CHAPTER 8

OTTAWA, CANADA

CANADIAN SECURITY INTELLIGENCE SERVICE (CSIS) headquarters is located at 1941 Ogilvie Road in Ottawa, the nation's capital.

Trees and green parkland surround the modern triangular shaped building. The view from his office was a nice one for Alexander Cuddy, Director of CSIS. Prime Minister Roger Hooper had only appointed him to the post a year ago and he was still adapting to his new role as Canada's security chief.

A former Royal Canadian Mounted Police officer, Cuddy had been involved in anti-espionage work with the RCMP until the government formed the new civilian spy agency in 1984. He then moved over to CSIS to continue his work. In recent years, counter terrorism activity became a priority for the agency.

Cuddy's phone rang. He picked up the receiver. "Cuddy here."

"Alex. It's Jim Knight at Langley. How are things in the tulip capital of Canada?" Knight was referring to the large number of tulips, which dotted the City of Ottawa – a gift from the Dutch for Canada's role in freeing the Netherlands from Nazi rule during the Second World War.

"Fine, Jim. At least until you called. I don't imagine this is a social call.

THE SCORPION

What's up?" Cuddy began doodling on a pad on his desk, a habit he developed whenever on the phone.

"Well, we have some Intel from one of our agents in Yemen that an operation may be underway targeting Canada. The Scorpion is heading it up. Something called Operation Saladin."

"What the hell is a Saladin?" Cuddy inquired.

Knight paused for a moment. Then he continued. "We think it's named after that twelfth century Muslim leader Salah ad-Din Yusuf ibn Ayyub, more commonly known as Saladin. He was the guy who defeated the Christians in the Holy Land Crusade and temporarily united the Muslim world."

"Do we know the target?"

"I'm afraid not, Alex. Our agent was discovered and killed before we got that information. But you can bet it must be big if the Scorpion is involved. Thought you should know so you can put your people on alert. If you need help, just ask. We'll put our resources at your disposal. I'd like to nail this bastard once and for all. Dead or Alive."

"Well, thanks for the tip, Jim, but I can't imagine a target they would be interested in up here. After all it's you guys, the Great Satan, they are more interested in hitting."

"That may be true. But you guys are right next door and our closest ally. I wouldn't underestimate them, Alex. If the Scorpion is involved, it is an important operation and one that may be designed to hurt us as much as it does you."

"True. Well, we'll put out an alert but we don't really know who we're looking for here. It would be nice if we had a photo or fingerprints of this Scorpion."

"Agreed. But this guy's as elusive as a fucking ghost. You need to be looking for a group of Arab-looking guys up to no good. I'd start by notifying your airport security. They will likely be arriving by plane."

"Right, Jim. Thanks for the Intel. We'll get right on it."

Cuddy disconnected the call. He couldn't help but think that his American cousins were just being their usual paranoid selves when it comes to terrorists. Although he couldn't blame them after 9/11. That tragic disaster was the result of some major internal security lapses. Overconfidence could breed big problems. Cuddy didn't want to fall into the same trap. So he decided it would be wise to put out a low-level alert to all agencies.

If Canada was a terrorist target – where did they plan to hit and what was their endgame?

CHAPTER 9

ST. LUKE'S HOSPITAL, TORONTO

THE LOBBY of St. Luke's Hospital teemed with people as Katie Cannon entered. She elbowed her way through a crowd of people to the information desk.

"Excuse me, I'm with the Daily Express….," Katie started to explain to the large, matronly woman seated behind the desk. She wore a hospital label that read: VOLUNTEER……Deborah Downie.

"The Press Conference is in Room 221A on the second floor," the volunteer curtly interrupted. "Elevators are over there on your right." She pointed in the direction of the elevators.

Katie moved in that direction, working her way around the crowd. Some of them were carrying placards and parading in a circle around the hospital lobby:

RIGHT TO LIFE FOR CHILDREN!

SAVE EMILY!

PRESERVE PARENTAL RIGHTS!

HOSPITALS SHOULDN'T BE KILLERS!

Two hospital security guards were standing nearby to ensure the protesters did not block access for visitors to the hospital.

Katie entered the elevator along with a couple of other people. She hit the number 2 button and within seconds stepped out into a long, brightly-lit hospital corridor. It must be the administrative wing. She noticed people in offices working on computers as she walked along the corridor to Room 221A.

Pushing open the door, Katie was greeted with the sight of a throng of reporters. Seated were several colleagues from competing papers with their notepads and mini-digital recorders. There were also radio and television reporters setting up microphones and cameras in front of a podium placed ahead of a St. Luke's Hospital banner with the hospital's name and logo.

"Hi there…..Sabrina Daniels, hospital PR," said a bubbly, blonde Thirty-something, offering her hand. "And you are?"

"Katie Cannon from the Daily Express." Katie shook the blonde's thin, bony hand.

"Well, welcome to St. Luke's. Here's your press kit." She handed over a thin folder containing a one-page news release and several sheets of background material on the hospital. "Please find a seat. The news conference will begin in a couple of minutes. There's coffee, muffins and donuts over by the wall."

"Thanks, I'm fine," replied Katie. She was watching her waistline these days, with the wedding only five days away. She didn't want to have problems fitting into her Vera Wang wedding gown.

After a few minutes, three people – two men and a woman -- entered the room from a side door and made their way to the podium.

"Could I have your attention please," said Sabrina Daniels. "The news conference is about to get underway." She introduced the three people on the podium: Benjamin Moore, chairman of the hospital board; Dr. Robert Bolton, chair of neurology and Linda Woodcock, coordinator of nursing.

Moore, a stocky man about six-foot tall, clean shaven and dressed in a dark blue business suit, stepped up to the podium microphone first. He held some note cards that he glanced at before speaking.

"Ladies and gentlemen of the press, thanks for your attention this morning. As most of you know we have an unfortunate situation where a three-year-old patient in our sick kids wing is currently on life support. She has a very rare irreversible neurological disease, which has left her in a vegetative state. Details are contained in your press kits.

"Needless to say, for the family and our hospital staff this has been a most tragic situation. Our sympathies go out to the family. Given the situation and the hopeless prognosis, it has reluctantly been the opinion of our senior medical staff, some of the top neurologists in the country, that nothing more can be done to treat little Emily. We have applied to the Province of Ontario's Consent and Capacity

Board to remove her breathing tube and allow nature to take its course. We feel it is in the best interests of the child although her parents do disagree with our decision. I have to announce this morning we received permission from the CCB yesterday."

Some members of the media immediately tried to ask questions, but Moore held up his right hand. "I would ask you to please hold all questions until we have finished this briefing. We will be happy to answer them then. At this time, I would like to call on our chief of neurology Dr. Robert Bolton to address some medical issues.

Bolton spoke for several minutes about details of the girl's brain disease. He was a thin, wiry man with silver streaked hair and a small goatee. He was in his 50s and wore a long, white lab coat.

Bolton summed up his comments and concluded: "Emily's parents have requested we perform a tracheotomy and send her home with them for whatever time she has left. But we feel this will just cause her prolonged pain and delay the inevitable. The Consent and Capacity Board agrees with our medical decision and we plan to continue with removal of life support as soon as possible."

Bolton introduced Linda Woodcock, the nursing coordinator, who addressed the kind of care Emily was receiving. She also conveyed the sympathy of the nursing staff to the family.

"But in the final analysis, we agree with the decision of her doctors that this is the best course of action and in the best interests of Emily……" said Woodcock.

"But why won't you respect the wishes of the family? Surely that should be paramount," shouted out one female reporter.

"Not at all," replied Dr. Bolton. "We must take into consideration what is in the best interests of our patient. We believe….."

At this moment, a man entering the room interrupted Bolton. He furiously waved a piece of paper.

"I have here a court order which overrules the Consent and Capacity Board's decision pending a judicial review," shouted the man in a gray, expensive looking Harry Rosen suit. "My name is Brian Bakker. My law firm is representing the family of Emily Carter. We intend to stop this hospital from killing this young girl."

Pandemonium broke out among the media people with this piece of breaking news.

CHAPTER 10

ROUTE 93, NEW HAMPSHIRE

THE DODGE CARAVAN continued north along Route 93. The lush green New Hampshire countryside rolled by as the vehicle moved along the tarmac.

Hashim Hadi drove with the Scorpion riding shotgun beside him in the front seat. There were three other men in the van, all part of the Operation Saladin team. Hadi was driving cautiously, staying close to the 55 mph speed limit. They did not want to risk being pulled over for speeding..

"How long until the Canadian border?" inquired the Scorpion.

"A couple of hours at least," replied Hadi.

"We are going to be too early. We must not arrive at the crossing site until late afternoon. You know the place?"

"Yes, we scouted it out. We can cross no problem. We just have to find some place to lay low until then."

"Good," said the Scorpion. He smiled. Things were going smoothly. Just as planned. He was a methodical man who believed that detailed planning was everything. The well-planned mission was usually a successful mission. Failure was not an option for him. He had never faced it. He wasn't about to start now.

THE SCORPION

Operation Saladin would strike a blow to the infidels never before seen.

*　*　*

Further back on Route 93, Deputy Sheriff Janet Cook drove her Ford Crown Victoria cruiser, enjoying the peaceful countryside. Her day so far had been quiet and uneventful except for a couple of traffic stops. One resulted in a warning and the other a ticket after the male driver made insulting and obnoxious comments to her.

Never a good idea to argue with an officer of the law. We have too many ways of putting you in your place, she thought.

Cook checked her wants and warrants and found an alert for a stolen SUV from Concord. There was also an alert from Homeland Security for a possible terrorist threat in the northeastern U.S. Any suspicious Arabic or Middle Eastern-looking groups needed to be checked out.

Chatter on the police radio was also quiet with only sporadic calls. Yes, it was a shaping up as a quiet, uneventful day. Cook was thankful. She hoped to get off shift early today to attend her 16-yar-old son Ian's concert solo at his school later this afternoon. Ian was a violinist and a talented one at that. Janet and her husband Ron, also a police officer, hoped their son might pursue a musical career. *Anything other than being a cop would be preferred*, she thought. Janet wanted a better and safer life for her son.

Her thoughts were of family as she entered the small town of Franklin. She checked her watch. 12:35 p.m. Time for lunch.

Ahead, Janet spotted a small roadside restaurant and decided to pull off. She eased into the parking lot and stopped her vehicle next to a Dodge Caravan parked in front of the restaurant, named Mary Ann's.

Yes, it is nice to have a quiet day for a change. Janet exited her vehicle and entered the restaurant.

CHAPTER 11

LONDON, ENGLAND

TREVOR TREVANIAN and Lynne Whitfield came out of the Majestic Theatre arm in arm. They enjoyed dinner earlier that evening and then the movie, *The King's Speech*, featuring Colin Firth and Geoffrey Rush.

Trevor, never one to socialize much with other journalists, found Lynne riveting, easy to talk to and not bad on the eyes. Actually, it had been a while since he had been with a woman. There were not many to date in Afghanistan, except whores. Trevor generally avoided them.

He was a little nervous around Lynne, not quite sure what he should do next. He didn't want to come on too strong. But he did find her attractive. That stirring in his loins was a clear signal.

"How about a nightcap? There's a nice pub just down the street," said Trevor.

Lynne gazed at him with those emerald green eyes. "Why don't we go back to my apartment instead? I have some beer and wine there. We'd be much more comfortable than in some musty old pub."

"Sounds good," replied Trevor. "I hope you're not going to take advantage of me. I don't usually get asked back to a girl's place on a first date."

"Ya never know. Just might be your lucky night!" Lynne flashed him a coy smile.

They located the nearest Tube station and caught a train to Lynne's apartment near the British Museum. It was in an old Georgian-style three-story walk-up.

"Nice place, very historic," said Trevor as he entered the living room. "And the Museum's only a few doors down."

"Afraid I don't get there much. Not one for museums. I prefer living in the present. Much more exciting." Lynne touched him lightly on his arm. Trevor felt an electric jolt. "Why don't you fix us a couple of drinks while I freshen up? Liquor's in the cabinet above the stove."

Lynne slid into her bedroom. She put her purse on the dresser. She opened it and removed the Walther PPK and placed it gently in a drawer in the night table next to her large Queen-size bed. It was covered with a duvet bearing various breeds of horses. She always slept with her gun nearby. *Never know when you are going to need it.*

She checked her face in the mirror and adjusted her blouse slightly to show a little more cleavage. She was used to seducing men, not a hard task. But she felt a bit uneasy about this. Her orders were to get closer to Trevor, but she actually was beginning to enjoy his company. He seemed a nice man for a journalist. He was easygoing, charming to talk with, and not unattractive in a physical sense. Trevor was a man who saw plenty of action in some interesting places in the world. Lynne found him quite a turn-on.

As she re-entered the living room, Trevor handed her a glass of white wine, while sipping on one himself.

"Not bad," he said. "Now where were we?"

"I think you were about to kiss me." Lynne put her glass down on a nearby coffee table and slipped into his waiting arms.

Trevor took her gently. Placing his own wine glass on the table, he slid his arms around her thin waist. He kissed her firmly on the lips. Moist, sensual. He felt as if he was drifting on a cloud. He pulled her closer to him. Their bodies entwined and melted together. Lynne felt the electric charge as he kissed her and returned his passion equally.

Without speaking, she led him into the bedroom. Lynne felt nothing at this moment but an overwhelming desire to possess this man.

CHAPTER 12
ONTARIO PROVINCIAL COURT #16

DONNA MARIE PIERCE took her seat in the media benches in Ontario Provincial Court #16. She was situated near the front just behind the defense attorney's table.

The courtroom was packed with spectators and media for the spectacle about to unfold. The high drama of a murder trial was guaranteed to generate high public and media interest. It was real life theatre at its best, despite the seriousness of the event.

Monica Porter faced second-degree murder charges for the Christmas Eve slaying of her husband, Malcolm. The morning session was taken up with interviews and selection of the jurors – 12 good citizens faced with the responsibility for deciding the guilt or innocence of the accused. Now the actual trial was about to begin in the afternoon session.

Monica Porter sat at the defense table next to her lawyer Clayton Evans, a tall, lanky man in his black robe. His silver hair shimmered in the neon light of the courtroom. Monica was a wisp of a thing. She appeared very slender, almost anorexic-looking in her stylish blue, floral dress. Next to her was Jeff Reynolds,

THE SCORPION

Evans's assistant attorney.

Directly across from them were the Crown Attorney's table and the prosecutors of the case. Alexander James, the Crown Attorney and his assistant Karmen Hunter sat behind a pile of documents on the table. James was a large, burly man who resembled Raymond Burr, the TV actor who played Perry Mason for many years in the 1960s. His assistant was in her 20s, raven-haired and wearing black spectacles. Despite the ugly black judicial robe, she seemed to have a knockout body.

Provincial Court Justice Deborah Livingstone banged her gavel to bring the court to order.

"Are you ready to proceed with your opening argument, Mr. James?"

"I am your Honor," said James, rising from his seat.

Donna Marie Pierce switched on her digital recorder and readied her pen to take notes as the proceedings started.

Walking to the jury panel, James looked squarely at the jurors and began his opening oration.

"Ladies and gentlemen of the jury, you are faced with the grave responsibility of bringing justice for Mr. Malcolm Porter, CEO and President of Metro Life Insurance. Over the next few days, the Crown will present evidence that the accused -- Mr. Porter's wife, Monica Porter, did murder her husband in a cold, calculating manner at a family dinner last Christmas Eve. We will present incontrovertible evidence that the accused callously committed this act in the presence of her children and other family members by shooting her husband and killing him.

Donna Marie jotted notes as James continued his oration for several minutes. After he finished, it was the defense attorney's turn. Clayton Evans slowly arose and calmly paced back and forth in front of the jury. He hooked his fingers into the lapels of his robe and began to speak:

"My esteemed colleague for the Crown is correct ladies and gentlemen in only one thing. My client did in fact shoot her husband on Christmas Eve and regrettably he died."

Some members of the jury seemed visibly shocked by Evans's candid admission.

"But I submit to you ladies and gentlemen of the jury that this act was not premeditated. Not a cold and calculated act as the Crown maintains. It occurred following a heated argument over circumstances from Mr. Porter's actions and infidelity over a long period of time, which created great mental stress and anguish for my client. She was not in sound mind when she committed this act. We will present evidence from an expert that clearly demonstrates this was an act of rage and passion. It was an irrational act of a heated moment and temporary insanity."

THE SCORPION

Wow, this going to be quite a story, thought Donna Marie as she hastily gathered her quotes.

She was eager to get back to the newsroom to file her story.

CHAPTER 13

FRANKLIN, NEW HAMPSHIRE

DEPUTY SHERIFF Janet Cook entered the small diner and made her way to a counter stool. She sat and turned on the stool to scout the room, as was her habit.

It was a busy place. The lunchtime crowd made a din with their chatter. Along the counter, men occupied four other stools. They silently read newspapers or checked their cell phones for messages.

People were seated at several tables in the small dining room. In the far corner, Cook observed one table with five men seated. She found it an interesting sight. They were a large group of Arabic-looking or Middle Eastern men eating their lunch, but not conversing. Cook thought it strange they would not be talking to each other.

"Hi Sheriff, what'll it be today? Would you like a menu?"

Cook turned to face a stout, middle-aged waitress behind the counter. She wore a nametag: Susan.

"No. I'll just have a toasted Denver sandwich and a coffee, Susie. Thanks."

"Coming right up. A Denver and coffee," said the waitress with a cheerful smile.

THE SCORPION

Cook turned back to the room. The Arabs were still quietly eating – no conversation at all. *Very strange. It's almost as if they are deliberately trying not to draw attention to themselves.*

Janet thought immediately of the Homeland Security alert. *These guys need to be checked out.*

She turned back to the counter so as not to tip the men off that they were being watched. Susan placed a coffee down and told Cook her sandwich would be up in a moment.

A couple of tables cleared, but the Arabs continued with their meal. They didn't seem to be in any hurry.

Fine, Janet decided. She didn't want to confront them here and would wait until they left the diner.

Soon her sandwich arrived and she began eating.

Several minutes later, another waitress went over to the table of the Arab men and Cook observed them paying their check. They were getting ready to leave. She wolfed down the rest of her sandwich and washed it down with the coffee.

As the men left the restaurant, she called Susan over.

"Hey, Susie. How much do I owe you? Duty calls, gotta run."

"It's on the house, Sheriff. Mack, the owner, doesn't believe in charging officers of the law."

"Fine, thanks." Janet left a $10 bill anyway. She wasn't comfortable accepting freebies.

As Janet left the diner, she observed the men getting into a Dodge Caravan and heading north on Route 93 toward Vermont.

She noted the license plate and called it in as soon as she entered the cruiser. She also told the dispatcher she was following the vehicle and planned to stop it and check it out.

"The vehicle is full of Middle Eastern men and is heading north. I plan to pull them over in accordance with Homeland Security memo #1278, terrorist alert," she stated calmly.

"Do you need back up?" replied the dispatcher.

"Not at this time. It's just a spot check. It may be nothing."

"Alright, but do be careful out there."

"Right. I'm always careful. 10-4 and out."

Janet Cook followed the Caravan for several miles along the highway into open countryside. Then she switched on her lights and siren, signaling the vehicle to pull over.

It did almost immediately, pulling onto the shoulder of the highway. Cook's cruiser parked right behind it.

THE SCORPION

She exited the vehicle and cautiously approached. As she did so, the passenger door on the Caravan opened and a tall man emerged. He walked quickly toward her, but appeared harmless. His hands were empty as he strolled toward her.

"Officer, is there some problem? I don't believe we were speeding. We are being most careful to stay within the law," said the man. He was tall, about 6-foot, two inches, lean and lanky and actually quite handsome, Janet thought. He had a warm smile on his face and appeared quite harmless. He was quite charming actually.

"Hold it right there, sir. Don't come any closer," Janet uttered sternly. "I didn't tell you to get out of your vehicle."

"Oh come on, Officer. Don't be so formal. We're minding our own business on our journey and you suddenly pull us over. What for? I'm simply trying to expedite matters here. We'd like to get on our way."

"Well, you can get on your way in a few moments, sir. There is no problem with speeding. This is just a random check. We have an alert out for some individuals like yourselves and I just need to check your identities. Where are you going?"

"We are on our way to Canada, actually. We're from Boston and heading to Vermont and Canada for a wedding in Quebec. There are five of us, brothers going to see our sister wed in Montreal."

"I see. May I see some identification, please? Then I will need your brothers to exit the vehicle and show me ID."

"Certainly. No problem, officer. I have my passport right here.' He tapped his side pocket. "May I take it out?"

"Yes, but do it slowly and keep your hands where I can see them." Cook walked closer to the man until she stood directly in front of him. He pulled out a U.S. passport and handed it to her. She checked the photo and ID. It appeared genuine.

"Tell me," the man smiled warmly. "Didn't I just see you back there at that roadside restaurant? The food was really good."

"Yes, it was," replied Janet who seemed satisfied at the passport that indicated the man was Abdul Halim, an American citizen from Boston. She was starting to feel easier about this. Perhaps they had nothing to do with the Homeland Security alert. "But I will need to see the identifications of your brothers. Do they also have passports?"

"Certainly. It will be no problem. I'll get them for you." Halim yelled in Arabic to the other men in the vehicle and they slowly began to emerge.

He then moved closer to Janet. "You are very beautiful, Officer. Are all female American police officers as alluring as you?"

THE SCORPION

By this time, he had positioned himself directly in front of her and very close to her body. His left hand moved behind his back and suddenly produced a knife. He grabbed the police officer and firmly held her struggling body.

"What the hell......" she cried.

Without hesitation, the Scorpion slashed quickly across her throat. He pushed her body away from him as a geyser of red erupted. Janet Cook fought to breathe as she felt the blood gurgling in her windpipe and she choked on her own lifeblood. She fell to the ground. Her final thoughts were of her husband Ron and son Ian.

Then she felt nothing.

"Such a pity. Such a waste," said the Scorpion gazing down at Janet's body. Still, she was only an infidel bitch. Collateral damage in the greater cause.

The Scorpion called out to his colleagues and two of the men carried her body to the long grass at the side of the road. They ditched it there like refuse.

The men then returned to the Dodge Caravan and the vehicle headed on its journey towards Vermont.

The police officer probably radioed in our license plate. We will need to change vehicles soon, especially after her body is discovered, the Scorpion decided. *Never mind, Allah will provide.*

CHAPTER 14

TORONTO DAILY EXPRESS

KATIE CANNON worked in her pod in the newsroom busily typing her story on the hospital situation. The newsroom was a hive of activity as reporters sat in their respective cubicles at their computers filing the day's stories.

The hospital news conference ended in chaos with the sudden announcement that the lawyers for the family of little Emily Carter would be challenging in court the hospital's decision to remove the breathing tube to end her life. That was the lead for Katie's story.

Seated next to her in the jammed newsroom, Donna Marie Pierce was writing her story on the murder trial. Her angle focused on the defense bid to get their client acquitted on grounds of temporary insanity. It was going to be an interesting trial.

Katie just finished up her copy when managing editor Braden Young approached her desk.

"Almost done, boss. Just wrapping up the story," said Katie.

"Sorry about this Katie, but I need you to get right back over to the hospital," said Young. He felt guilty because he knew Katie was busy finalizing details for her wedding this weekend. "There are some new developments in the Emily Carter story."

"What on Earth now? Isn't a court challenge enough?"

"There's been a bomb threat. Some yahoo sent in a note protesting that the hospital is a baby killer. He's threatening to blow the whole place sky high!"

CHAPTER 15
DERBY LINE, VERMONT

IT WAS late afternoon when the Dodge Caravan entered the sleepy Vermont town of Derby Line, with a population of about 800.

The town straddles the border of the USA and Canada, just across from Stanstead, Quebec, less than 100 miles southeast of Montreal. The town offered a unique challenge to border security officials because the border passes through the streets of both towns and in many cases through the buildings and houses. A family in some houses can cook dinner in a kitchen in the United States and eat the meal in the dining room in Canada.

The Scorpion knew the town well. He had thoroughly researched it on the Internet and knew that if they were careful his party could cross easily into Canada without being questioned by border officials.

The van pulled onto a small side street and the Scorpion ordered the driver Hashim Hadi to park the vehicle. It was time to abandon the van and become pedestrians.

The five occupants exited the Caravan and started walking through the town. The Scorpion led them along the sidewalk past some of the side streets where security gates had been installed to block access to Canada.

U.S. and Canadian border officials did this in 2009 over the objections of residents in both towns to try to limit the easy crossings as part of post 9/11 tightening of the borders. Security cameras and ground sensors were installed in other areas to monitor traffic.

It was not unusual for a person to inadvertently wander over the line and minutes later be descended upon by border agents. Signs were posted at many crossing points telling people to report to the nearest border inspection post.

The Al-Qaeda group headed towards a large brick building. The Scorpion knew this was the Haskell Free Library and Opera House. It was deliberately constructed on the international border and opened in 1904.

The donors were Carlos Haskell, an American businessman who owned a number of sawmills and his wife Martha Stewart Haskell, a Canadian philanthropist. It was intended that people on both sides of the border would have free use of the facility, now a designated historic site.

The Scorpion also knew that patrons of the library from either side of the border may use it without going through border security. The entrance is on the U.S. side of the border.

The men entered the library and saw a reading room with shelves lined with books, a hardwood floor and several tables with patrons seated at them. The

Scorpion nodded and gave a warm smile to the matronly, middle-aged librarian seated behind a counter. Two other librarians were working in the background.

The men spread out and wandered around the library. Some picked up books and browsed, while others just wandered around the building. The Scorpion walked over a strip of black electrical tape running across the room, which marked the border into Canada where most of the books were shelved.

They spent about an hour inside the library killing time to make it appear like they were genuine patrons for any border patrol agents who may be watching outside.

The Scorpion checked his watch. 5:35 p.m. He signaled the others that it was time to leave.

"I will go first and you all follow about five minutes apart," he told them. "It will appear more normal that we cross as individuals rather than as a group. It will draw less attention to us by anyone who may be watching the monitors. Remember, just walk along Church Street next to the library. It is only a few steps into Canada. We will meet at a café on the other side called The Meridian."

The Scorpion headed out first. He turned the corner onto Church Street. He walked calmly and confidently for a few hundred yards. He noticed the security cameras perched atop light poles. He stopped momentarily at a white line painted across the street. North of the line it read CANADA, south of it, USA. The

THE SCORPION

Scorpion smiled and stepped across the line. He headed for The Meridian nearby without challenge.

* * *

Twenty minutes later, the five men were seated in the café. All made the crossing safely into Canada without incident.

Such fools, these North Americans. They are so easily duped. It will not be long before Islam rules here and over the entire Earth, the Scorpion thought.

They decided to have dinner here. A swarthy, middle-aged man, of obvious Middle Eastern descent approached their table, carrying menus.

"Welcome to my humble café, brothers. I am Ibrahim Hafcz, owner of this establishment. We serve the finest Mediterranean cuisine."

"Are you of the faith, brother?" inquired the Scorpion.

"Most certainly. May Allah be with us always! I am Palestinian and came here to Canada seven years ago as a refugee. Now I am a successful businessman and have a safe country to raise my family."

"That is good. We also are new to this country and are seeking to make our mark."

"Welcome. If you work hard, you will be most successful."

"That is exactly what we are hoping. Our objective is success that will transform this country."

"May Allah grant your wishes. Now what would you like to order?"

The men ordered their meals. The Scorpion decided their next step must be to acquire a new vehicle to carry them on the rest of their journey and their mission.

CHAPTER 16
ST. LUKE'S HOSPITAL

AS KATIE CANNON approached the main entrance to St. Luke's Hospital she saw a parade of people and placards circling out front. The police had moved all the protesters outside as part of their enhanced security measures in the wake of the bomb threat.

When she entered the front doors, a security officer confronted her and carefully perused her press credentials before admitting her to the premises. Security had really been tightened.

Within minutes, Katie met with Sabrina Daniels, the hospital's PR person, in Daniels's office. Daniels gave her the lowdown on the threatening note the hospital had been sent.

"Can I see the note?" asked Katie.

"I'm afraid not," said Sabrina. "The note has been given to the police to see if they can track down its origin. It is now evidence. But I can tell you it gave a diatribe about the sanctity of life and the need to save baby Emily's life. It threatened to blow up the hospital unless all efforts are made to prolong her life."

"But that's crazy! Doesn't the person realize that a bomb might also kill

Emily in the process? And what about the lives of other people in the hospital? It's not rational."

"There's no rationality with some of these nutbars out there. It's just like some of the fanatic pro-lifers who firebomb abortion clinics. I don't think reasoning comes into the equation with these people." Sabrina ran her thin fingers through her long, blonde hair. She seemed very stressed out to Katie. No wonder.

"Do the police have any leads?"

"I'm not sure. You'll have to ask them. They haven't told us if they have. There are plenty of them patrolling the hospital along with our security staff."

"Well thanks, Sabrina. You've been very helpful. Let's just hope it's a harmless prank."

As Katie walked out of Sabrina's ground floor office, she spied a trio of police officers at the Tim Hortons counter getting coffee and donuts. One of them was very familiar to her. It was Detective Peter Moon. She had worked extensively with him on many cases and he was the man who had rescued her from the clutches of the Wolfman, the serial killer who abducted her last year.

"Hey, Katie. Come over here." Moon gestured to her when he spotted her. He was a tall, lean, beach boy blonde. Very handsome. "Would you like a coffee?"

"Sure. I'll take a large, double-double."

THE SCORPION

Moon got their two coffees and they sat at one of the small tables in the lobby.

"So, have they got you on the hospital bomber story?" he asked.

"Yep. So why is one of Toronto's top homicide dicks on the bomber case?"

"Well, we're very shorthanded just now, what with summer vacations and all, so they thought I could lend a hand with my vast expertise of homicidal maniacs."

"Got any leads on the bomber yet?"

"Nope. But we've got lots of police covering the hospital. We hope to catch this nutcase if he actually tries to do anything."

"Any good at defusing bombs if you catch him Peter?"

"Not me. But we have Bomb Disposal on standby just in case."

"What do you think your chances are if he does try?"

"If he tries anything, there's a pretty good chance we'll catch him in the act. But personally I think it's probably just a prank letter. No real threat."

Katie only hoped Peter Moon was right.

DAY THREE

TUESDAY

CHAPTER 17

LONDON, ENGLAND

THE SUN arose over London, its rays streaming over the River Thames, the Tower Bridge, the Houses of Parliament, Westminster Abbey and bounced off the silver dome atop St. Peter's Cathedral.

The sunshine beamed through Lynne Whitfield's bedroom window and bathed the two forms lying in the Queen-size bed with its glow. Trevor and Lynne stirred. She lay nestled in close to him. Trevor thought back to last night and the wonderful passion they enjoyed.

Sure beats Afghanistan.

He arose from the bed and glanced at the small alarm clock on the oak bedside table. 7:15 a.m. He padded to the bathroom. Performed Nature's calling and then ran the shower. He stepped in and allowed the luxurious needles of hot water to massage his body.

He stood there several minutes enjoying the spray when the shower curtain parted and he felt a body slip in next to him.

"Feel like some company?" purred Lynne. She picked up a wash cloth and gently moved it over his body, scrubbing him gently. She moved lower and lower.

Trevor felt a faint stirring in his loins that grew as she continued with her ministrations.

He turned and pulled her close to him. He kissed her powerfully, rubbing his hands down her wet back and her beautiful ass. They made passionate love as the needles of water continued to pound down on them.

* * *

"That was some shower," observed Trevor as he toweled himself off.

"It was rather invigorating," said Lynne. "And rather nice. How about some breakfast? Bacon and eggs?"

"Sounds fine. You've worked up quite an appetite for me."

Later as Trevor sat at the kitchen table eating his bacon and eggs and munching on whole-wheat toast, he turned to Lynne and commented: "You know you're quite a woman, Lynne. It was very fortunate your heel broke when it did, otherwise we might never have met."

"Karma, I guess," replied Lynne.

"Listen, Lynne. I'd like to get to know you much better but I have to leave tomorrow. I'm flying to Toronto to attend the wedding of my boss this weekend. Any chance you could come along? You could be my date for the wedding."

"Hmmm. Sounds interesting. It may be a possibility. I'll ask my boss at work today. I'm owed some time off. Don't see why I can't take a few days now.

I've never been to Canada. It might be fun!"

"Right then, I'll take that as a yes. I have to get back to my apartment to do some more work on my book, but I'll call and book an extra ticket. I'll also get us a room at the Westin Harbor Castle on the waterfront; it's only a short walk to the reception at the CN Tower. You'll love it and I can show you the city."

"Sounds great, Trevor. That is if we ever leave the hotel room." Lynne winked at him with a mischievous smile.

After Trevor left the apartment, Lynne picked up her mobile and hit the speed dial.

"This is Gemini reporting in. I have established a close rapport with the contact. I will be accompanying him to Toronto tomorrow."

"Excellent," said the voice on the other end of the phone. "Stay close and monitor him. Report in after you arrive in Toronto."

She closed the flip phone. She was only carrying out her duty, but why did she feel so bad about it?

CHAPTER 18

TORONTO DAILY EXPRESS

THE EDITORS gathered in the news conference room for their morning story meeting. It was the daily session where they gathered to discuss the breaking news stories of the day and what their reporters were working on.

Also, like Knights of the Round Table they would joust over placing of the stories in the next day's paper and who would get the coveted front-page slots.

Braden Young, as managing editor, presided over the meeting and tried to keep order. Sometimes, he felt like he was refereeing a hockey game. Arguments would often break out as editors passionately argued the case for their various stories and served as advocates for their reporters.

"Let's get this show on the road, people. We're all very busy. What are we looking at for top line tomorrow?" Young asked.

"I would think there is no doubt our top story is the bomb threat at St. Luke's over the Emily Carter case," said Paul O'Connor, assistant managing editor. "Police are tightening security at the hospital and Katie Cannon is working on an updated story as we speak."

"Right, Paul. I think that's a good call. There's great public interest in this story. It brings out both sides of this ethical debate for the medical community. I don't think there is any doubt we have anything that tops this story right now. Anyone disagree?"

The other editors shook their heads silently.

Michael Owen, the paper's city editor, suddenly piped up. "We also have that murder trial of the wife that shot her husband Christmas Eve. Donna Marie Pierce is covering that one. It should provide us with some juicy copy, especially since he was screwing around on her.

"Not sure that's page one material at this point, Mike," said Braden. "We'll see what else develops. Perhaps slot it for top of page 3 for now."

Ted Morrow, the national editor, said: "We have a Gallup poll story that says President Obama's approval rating has sunk to an all-time low – 38 per cent. Experts say he needs at least 48 percent or higher if he expects to be re-elected. He has requested time to address a joint session of Congress to talk about job creation and his economic recovery plan. I think it's worthy of front-page consideration. I ...."

"Bullshit!" interrupted Owen. "Who the hell gives a fuck up here that the American economy is in the toilet. Inside stuff at best and it's only a fucking poll. Dogs know what to do with polls."

"A lot of people are interested, you moron. If they're not, they should be,"

Morrow snapped back. "The U.S. is our biggest trading partner. If the American economy goes in the toilet, Canada's is likely to follow. That's what you get when you sleep next to an elephant."

"OK, guys, let's cool your jets," said Braden stepping into the dispute. "No need for name-calling, Ted. You're right about the importance of the story. Not sure the poll is front page worthy, Ted, but Obama's address to Congress and the Republican reaction sure will be. Let's look at it for page 2 for now. What do we have on the international scene, Amanda?"

Amanda Scott, the paper's international affairs editor, was doodling on a notepad. She put down her pen and looked up as Braden addressed her.

"We have a couple of great stories shaping up," she said. "An earthquake has rocked Japan. Reports of casualties so far have been low. Apparently there is extensive property damage and blackouts in Tokyo, Nagasaki, Kyoto and other areas on the island. We don't have a true picture of all the damage yet as blackouts and communications are down in many places. But our Asian correspondent Mark Reaney is on the story."

"Good. We can play that top line in our International Section," said Braden.

"We also have an update on the trouble in Syria," added Scott. " Bashar al-Assad's forces are trying to crush the opposition to his regime and killing thousands, including innocent women and children. That bastard's trying to hang on to power at all costs. And the UN is considering further sanctions against Syria."

"Great. Play that second line, Amanda."

Braden turned to Alexandra Stewart, the entertainment editor, smiling: "And what do we have on the entertainment scene, Alexandra. Hopefully something cheerful for our readers after all this other shit."

"We try, Braden. We try. Actually we have an advance on this year's Toronto Film Festival this September. Some big names will attend. Already confirmed are Brad Pitt, Angelina Jolie, George Clooney, Megan Fox, Canadians Ryan Gosling and Rachel MacAdams, and many other stars. TIFF is becoming one of the top film festivals, rivaling Cannes."

"That's great news for the city. People really lap up all this celebrity stuff. Give it generous play, Alexandra. What about the world of sports, Steve?"

Steve Simons, the paper's portly sports editor, put down the donut he was munching on. "Right Braden. The Blue Jays open a three-day home stand against the Yankees tonight. At this point, they can only act as spoilers in the East division race. They are in fifth place, 18 games behind the Yankees who are first, two and a half games ahead of Boston Red Sox. We also have word of a major off-season trade shaping up between the Toronto Maple Leafs and Chicago Blackhawks. There's never a dull moment in the world of jocks."

"A bunch of overpaid kids for just playing games, if you ask me," commented Paul O'Connor.

"Perhaps," replied Simons. "But sports are big business these days and it keeps the masses entertained. Helps keep our minds off all this other depressing shit in the paper."

"Right. On that note I think that concludes our business today," said Braden. "We'll meet this afternoon for our final story wrap and placement. That's all folks!"

The editors all departed the room. They headed back to business in the busy newsroom.

Braden checked the clock. 9:15 a.m.

He has a medical appointment with a Urology specialist at 1:30 p.m., but he needs to pick up Leah. He wants her with him when he gets the news of his prostate biopsy. Hopefully it will be good news, but Braden somehow feels a sense of nagging uncertainty.

CHAPTER 19
ONTARIO PROVINCIAL COURT #16

AS THE COURT proceedings began, Donna Marie Pierce started taking notes and had her trusty digital recorder running.

The prosecuting Crown Attorney Alexander James questioned his first witness, Detective Inspector Alan Jones. He was the homicide detective who headed up the Porter murder investigation.

"Inspector Jones, would you please tell this court what you observed when you responded to the 911 call last Christmas Eve."

"Certainly. I was dispatched to the scene after uniformed officers who responded to the initial call determined that a shooting death had occurred. When I arrived, family members at the dinner party were all present. Mr. Porter, the victim was slumped in his seat with a single gunshot wound to the chest. It was a fatal wound. The autopsy later determined he had been hit in the heart. Mrs. Porter was crying and in custody of two officers when I arrived."

"And what action did you take then?"

"Well, I interviewed members of the family -- the married son and daughter and their respective spouses. They confirmed that the family had been having Christmas dinner. During the course of it a heated argument arose between Mr. and

Mrs. Porter. Mrs. Porter stormed out of the room. A few minutes later, she returned to the room. She possessed a handgun and calmly approached Mr. Porter, aimed the gun and fired a single shot."

"Objection, your Honor." Defense Attorney Clayton Evans jumped to his feet. "The witness is making a judgment of Mrs. Porter's state of mind. He is not qualified to make that claim that she calmly approached Mr. Porter."

"Sustained," said Judge Deborah Livingstone. Turning to Jones, she added, "Please confine your testimony to the facts, Inspector. The jury will disregard that last comment and take into consideration only that Mrs. Porter approached the victim and fired a single shot."

"Then what happened, Inspector?" inquired James.

"We had Forensics gather evidence. Then Mrs. Porter was arrested and taken into custody for further questioning."

"Was she advised of her rights?"

"Yes, sir. She was also advised that she could have a lawyer present during questioning and she requested one. Her interview was delayed until Mr. Evans arrived. I believe the family retained him on her behalf."

"And what did she say during that interview?"

"Not too much, I'm afraid. Mrs. Porter was quite distressed. She was very teary and not too communicative. I believe she was in shock."

"Did she admit to shooting, Mr. Porter?"

"Not per se. She talked a lot about his infidelity, the fact that she gave him 30 years of her life and that he had left her for a younger woman. She was in a very distressed state."

"Thank you Inspector. That will be all."

After James sat down, the Judge offered Evans the chance for cross-examination.

"Thank you, your Honor," said Evans who crossed in front of Detective Inspector Jones in the witness box and stared directly at him. "Inspector Jones, you stated that Mrs. Porter was in a distressed frame of mind. How bad was she? Did she seem rational?"

"Objection, your Honor." Crown Attorney James was back on his feet. "Calls for the witness to make a judgment of which he is not qualified."

"Sustained. Confine yourself to facts, Mr. Evans."

"Certainly, your Honor. My apologies. Let me ask you this, Inspector. Would you say that Mrs. Porter was in a traumatic state?"

"Your Honor!" James objected.

"Overruled. I think that is a fair question as to her condition observed at the time of questioning. I will allow it."

"Mrs. Porter obviously had suffered great trauma and was not in a very coherent state when we tried to interview her. We suspended the interview until the next day, as you well know Mr. Evans."

"Yes. During that second interview, was Mrs. Porter in a better frame of mind?"

"Yes, much better. She was calmer and more collected and answered our questions in your presence."

"Did she in fact admit to the shooting at that time?"

"In a sense, yes. She admitted she must have shot him but she did not remember it."

"Thank you, Inspector Jones." Evans felt he had scored a relevant point.

The trial continued throughout the morning with the prosecution bringing forward several more witnesses, including Porter family members to describe what happened that fateful Christmas Eve night,

At 12:35 p.m. the judge adjourned for lunch.

CHAPTER 20

MONTREAL, QUEBEC

THE FIVE MEN left the Fleuer de Lis Motel on the outskirts of Montreal in a brand new blue Ford Escape.

The Scorpion had considered highjacking a new vehicle for the group, but he felt that it was too risky. If the vehicle was reported stolen, the license plate would be circulated among law enforcement agencies. He thought it safer to rent a vehicle in Stanstead and the small SUV suited their purposes perfectly.

They drove to Montreal that night and booked into the shabby motel. Now they were headed to the docks to rendezvous with their contact and to pick up their shipment.

It was just after noon when they pulled into the docks area and parked outside one of the large warehouses. The five men entered the warehouse, which appeared empty. They waited several minutes. Soon another figure appeared in the shadowy doorway.

The man walked toward them carrying a small briefcase. He appeared to be a merchant seaman, with a large black beard and was wearing jeans, a red and blue checked shirt and a cap.

"Allah be praised," he said. "You made it safely."

"And may he bless you, brother," replied the Scorpion. "I trust your journey was uneventful."

"The freighter arrived two days ago. The journey was good. No problems."

"Is that the package?" The Scorpion pointed to the briefcase in the man's hand.

"It is. It just needs to be armed when you arrive at the target. It is perfectly safe to carry. Just don't jostle it around too much."

"Good. You have done well my brother and your actions will advance the cause of Islam. Your contribution will long be remembered after our attack on the infidels."

The Scorpion took the briefcase carefully and stared upon it.

Now we have the means to deliver a devastating blow. They will never recover from this. The Twin Towers will pale in comparison.

The Scorpion held all the power in his hands. The briefcase was a suitcase nuke.

CHAPTER 21

SUNNYBROOK HOSPITAL, TORONTO

BRADEN YOUNG and Leah McCall sat silently in the waiting room of the Urology department. They held hands. Leah caressed Braden's arm gently. She could sense his apprehension.

Soon a nurse appeared and called: "Mr. Young, Dr. Bock will see you now."

Moments later Braden and Leah were in a small room with an examination table, a metal desk with a computer on it and a couple of chairs.

"Good afternoon, Mr. Young," said a middle-aged man in a white coat entering the room. His nametag read Dr. Reginald Bock. "Nice to see you again. How are you doing?"

"Fine, Doc. This is Leah, my girlfriend. She's an RN. I brought her along to help me understand your medical mumbo jumbo."

"That's OK. It often helps to have someone along to help you comprehend the information. We now have the results of your biopsy. I'm afraid that I have good news and bad news for you, Mr. Young. The bad news is you do have prostate cancer. But the good news is that it has been caught at a very early stage and is highly treatable. Your family doctor was right on top of the situation in referring you to us for a biopsy after your elevated PSA test results."

The news hit Braden like a lightning bolt. The Big C. His worst fear. His body suddenly went numb and he had trouble concentrating on the words coming from the doctor's mouth. Leah squeezed his hand tighter.

"Your cancer is only in Stage One. I repeat it is highly treatable and there is a 95 percent cure rate at that level. One in six men over 40 will develop prostate cancer. The stats are very similar to breast cancer in women. I must repeat, Mr. Young, this is not a death sentence and you have an outstanding prognosis if it is treated soon. Prostate cancer is also a very slow growing cancer and you could go years before it causes you any problems. You're still not suffering any symptoms such as urinary pain or blood in your urine?"

"No, I feel fine. Except I sometimes have to pee more frequently."

"Excellent. You're in very good shape, Mr. Young. You have an outstanding chance to beat this thing and have many good years ahead of you."

"What are you recommending for treatment, doctor?" inquired Leah.

"Well there are basically three options. The first is what we call Watch and Wait – do nothing at this time and continue to monitor you every few months to observe the cancer. But that would mean constant checkups and periodic biopsies to see how fast the cancer is developing. We usually only recommend this approach to people in their 80s because they are likely to die from something else long before the cancer becomes a problem.

"The second option would be targeted radiation therapy to try to kill the cancer. We literally fry the prostate gland. The results are pretty high with this option.

"The third option, and the one I would recommend, is surgery to remove the prostate gland. It would be laparoscopic surgery performed with a robotic arm. It's much less invasive and would require a hospital stay of about three days and one month's recovery at home. It also offers the highest guarantee of success by cutting out the cancer before it can spread. I would strongly recommend that option. But if you prefer to try radiation therapy, we can refer you to an oncologist."

"Wow. This is all a bit overpowering," said Braden. He appeared dazed and had trouble taking in all the information. "I hope I don't have to make a decision today. I'd like some time to consider the options."

"No problem, Mr. Young. There is no hurry. Take a few days to mull it over, discuss it with your girlfriend and do some research. We can give you some literature from the Cancer Society and some Web addresses where you can find more information. Take some time to weigh the pros and cons and give us a call in a week or two and we will set things up for you. Just don't leave it too long. You need to take action on this fairly soon to nip the problem in the bud. Are there any other questions I can answer?"

Braden hesitated for a moment, then asked: "What about sex? Will this surgery put an end to that?"

"Well, impotence is a side effect of both surgery and radiation, as well as incontinence. The laparoscopic surgery spares the nerve damage from normal surgery but it still causes some temporary impotence. Most men are usually able to resume sexual function within a year or two. We also have treatments to aid you in this. You will also have to put up with a catheter for about two weeks after surgery and wear pads until you regain urinary control. Again, we can help you with this through certain exercises."

"I don't know about this...." Braden looked at Leah.

"Don't worry about it darling. We will get through this together. I would rather have you alive." She gently patted his arm reassuringly and gave him a hug.

"Well, I'd like to think about it some more, doc. I'll get back to you."

"That's perfectly understandable, Mr. Young. You have a lot to consider. Just let me know when you are ready and we'll get the ball rolling."

Leah helped Braden out of the examination room as they re-entered the waiting room. It had been quite a shock for him. Braden now faced some major life changing decisions.

CHAPTER 22

MONTREAL, QUEBEC

THE SCORPION and his four colleagues huddled in front of the Ford Escape.

"It is now time for us to separate for our missions, brothers," said the Scorpion still holding his deadly briefcase. "Hashim, you will lead this phase of Operation Saladin. First you will drop Ali and I at the train station where we will depart for our operation. Then you take Khaled and Shareet to Ottawa to join our other colleagues there for that phase of your operation. You know the target and what needs to be done. May Allah be with you!"

"And with you, brother," said Hadi.

Hadi drove to downtown Montreal and dropped the Scorpion and Ali Saleh off at the VIA train station. They then departed on the road to Ottawa, Canada's capital city.

The Scorpion purchased two first-class tickets to Toronto. He and Saleh sat in the waiting room until the call for their 500-mile journey to their destiny and glory. The briefcase stood like a sentinel next to the Scorpion's feet.

CHAPTER 23

ST. LUKE'S HOSPITAL, TORONTO

THREE FLOORS UP, a man in a doctor's white coat with a stethoscope around his neck, walked past the Nurse's station carrying a small briefcase. He walked with determination. He was a man on a mission.

The doctor strode along the corridor, past patient rooms until he came to a storage room.

He entered the room and found it stacked with various medical supplies and equipment. He brought up the briefcase and opened it.

Inside, the case was packed with plastic explosives attached to a detonator and several wires. The digital timer at the side read 0:00. The man tinkered with the timer and set it at 2:00. It started to count down. 1:59. 1:58. 1:57....

Two hours. It was plenty of time to get clear of the hospital.

Malcolm Wilkes had been an explosives expert in the army. He was a Born Again Christian who strongly opposed abortion and had bombed a couple of clinics to send a message to these baby killers.

He had seen the stories about what St. Luke's was doing to little Emily and her family. She just wanted a chance to live and breathe and spend what little time she had left with her family at home. Surely that was not too much to ask.

He needed to send a strong message to the hospital. He didn't want to hurt anyone. He planned to phone the hospital once he got clear and they would have plenty of time to evacuate patients. If they agreed to perform the tracheotomy, he would tell them where the bomb was located and it could be defused.

He slowly closed the lid on the briefcase and slipped it in with the other equipment in the storage room.

Wilkes headed back down the corridor. As he passed an in-patient room, a nurse came rushing out. Her nametag read: Louise Matthews.

"Doctor,,,,,,in here, STAT. We need your help. A patient is in cardiac arrest," she said with urgency. "We need a crash cart now in Room 316," she hollered down the hallway. She grabbed the doctor by his arm, pulling him into the room.

The male patient lay on the bed hooked up to various monitors. Lights flashed. Buzzers were sounding. The patient's face was a turning a bluish tinge.

Wilkes just stood there helpless. He was frozen just staring at the man on the bed.

"Come on doctor, do something. The patient is dying." Matthews looked at Wilkes and was baffled at his inaction. *Something is definitely wrong here. This doctor is acting like an intern facing his first crisis.*

At that moment, two other nurses and another doctor entered the room with a crash cart. They immediately set to work hooking up the defibrillator to the patient's chest and started to administer electric shocks.

Wilkes started backing to the door.

Matthews grabbed him by the arm. "Just who are you doctor? Why aren't you wearing a nametag?"

Wilkes pushed her violently backward and ran out the door.

"Wait," cried Matthews. "I'm calling the police."

* * *

As Katie Cannon sat chatting with Inspector Peter Moon and drinking coffee at a table near the Tim Hortons counter in the lobby, Moon's cell phone rang.

He answered and suddenly jumped up. He approached the two uniformed police officers stationed in the lobby. "Right guys, we have a report of a possible fake doctor on the third floor. He fled the scene and may be making his way out of the hospital. He directed the two men to cover the nearest stairwells. "I'll take the main elevator."

Moon moved in front of the bank of public elevators and Katie joined him.

Within seconds a bell sounded. The doors of the center elevator opened and three people walked out. There were two women and a doctor wearing a white coat.

THE SCORPION

Moon immediately noticed the man in the white coat wasn't wearing any ID. "Excuse me, sir I need to talk with you a ….."

The man ran. Moon followed in hot pursuit.

After a few yards, he made a flying leap and tackled the fugitive doctor around his ankles. They both hit the carpeted floor hard. Wilkes struggled furiously, but Moon overcame him and soon was assisted by the two uniformed police officers. Within minutes, Wilkes was subdued and handcuffed.

"Right, it appears we have our man. Now, who are you and what are you doing in this hospital?" said Moon.

Wilkes said nothing.

Three floors above, the bomb continued its countdown. 1:40…1:39…1:38.

CHAPTER 24

ONTARIO PROVINCIAL COURT #16

THE PORTER murder trial resumed after lunch.

The prosecution produced witnesses to testify to the marital breakdown of the couple. They pointed out that Malcolm Porter had left his wife and was co-habiting with his much younger secretary. Witnesses testified that the breakup had been hard on Monica Porter and there had been frequent arguments over his affair and now his new live-in relationship.

Malcolm only returned to their house for official family engagements. And that included the family Christmas Eve gathering where his wife shot him.

"My next witness, Your Honor is Dr. Gabriel Stableford," said Alexander James, the Crown Attorney.

Stableford, a middle-aged, balding man with only a wisp of hair around the edge of his scalp, took the stand and the oath.

"Dr. Stableford. Please tell this court your occupation."

"I am a clinical psychiatrist and consult with the police on many cases."

"And are you familiar with the accused, Mrs. Monica Porter?"

"I am. I was called in by the police to interview Mrs. Porter and conduct a thorough psychiatric evaluation."

"And what did you conclude from that interview, Dr. Stableford?"

Stableford hesitated a moment to collect his thoughts. "After three interviews, I concluded that Mrs. Porter is of sound mental health, knows the difference between right and wrong, is cognizant of the seriousness of her current situation and has some remorse for her actions. She is a highly traumatized individual who has been devastated by the breakup of her marriage. She also feels a deep sense of betrayal by her husband and believes she has been cast aside for a younger woman."

"Thank you, Dr. Stableford. Now would it be fair to assume that this deep sense of betrayal was a cause for her actions in shooting her husband? Did she in fact know what she was doing when she shot him?"

"Yes. And it is my considered professional opinion that although agitated, she knew exactly what she was doing when she pulled that trigger."

James smiled. *This case is a slam dunk.* "Thank you, Dr. Stableford. Your witness, Mr. Evans."

Clayton Evans strode to the witness box and paced silently in front of it. He seemed deep in thought as if contemplating how to proceed. He cleared his throat and then began.

"Dr. Stableford, how many cases have you consulted on with the police?"

"Well, that would be hard to say," Stableford scratched his head as if trying to pull the number out of his brain. I'm not exactly sure. But I know it has been very many over several years. I'm not sure how many, but a lot."

Evans pulled a small piece of paper out of his pocket. "Would it surprise you if I told you that you have testified 102 times for the prosecution?"

"No. That would sound about right."

"And how many of those have you found insane or suffering from temporary insanity?"

"I have no idea, sir. There have been too many cases. I suppose at least several of them. Statistically that would be possible," replied Stableford curtly.

"What if I told you there were only two cases of insanity that you found? Two cases out of 102."

"Objection, your Honor," shouted James rising to his feet. "Where has learned counsel come up with these figures and what relevance are they?"

"These figures come from court records, your Honor and are accurate. They point to the testimonial record of the witness and that he often tells the prosecution what they want to hear. The two cases of insanity were so extreme even he couldn't ignore them."

"There is relevance here, Mr. James. I will allow this," Judge Livingston ruled.

"And are you compensated for your time by the Crown, sir?" asked Evans.

"Certainly I am paid a consulting fee for each case. I don't work for free. Do you, Mr. Evans?"

"Sometimes, Dr. Stableford. I do pro bono work for needy clients. But isn't it fair to say you make a good living from your consulting with the police and prosecution, so it is in your best interests to given them the results they needed?"

"I object to your insinuations, sir!" said Stableford haughtily.

"Your Honor!" cried James. "This is an outrageous allegation by the defense."

Livingstone looked stony-f aced at Evans. "Proceed cautiously, here, Mr. Evans. You are on very shaky ground. Be careful about accusations of any misconduct." She turned to the jury panel. "Members of the jury will ignore that last comment by the defense counsel."

Evans was satisfied. He had made his point to the jury.

"That is all the questions I have for Dr. Stableford, your Honor."

"Thank you. Any redirect, Mr. James?"

"Just one, your Honor," replied James rising again. " Dr. Stableford , did you give your honest professional opinion in all those 102 cases?"

"I certainly did!"

"Thank you for your testimony today. I have no further questions."

"Your next witness please, Mr. James," stated the Judge.

James was confident he had made a solid case and that the win was in the bag. He had no need of further witnesses.

"Your Honor, the Crown rests its case."

Judge Livingstone looked at the clock on the wall and saw it was late afternoon. 4:15 p.m. "Given the time, we will adjourn today and resume tomorrow when the defense will present its case."

She banged her gavel on the desk and court adjourned.

CHAPTER 25

BRADEN YOUNG'S APARTMENT

THE NEWS had hit Braden Young hard.

The Big C.

Why me? Why now? What is all this going to mean for my life, my career and my relationship with Leah, just when things are going great?

Leah sat with him in the apartment, holding him, comforting him and just trying to be supportive as Braden came to grips with the devastating news he had received. She made them coffee and they sipped on it with some shortbread biscuits she found in a cupboard.

Braden had called in to the newspaper saying he wouldn't be back today. He left today's paper in the capable hands of Paul O'Connor.

"Look Braden, I know this was rough news to get, but we have to stay positive," said Leah. "The news is really very good. They caught it early and you have an excellent chance of beating this."

"Yeah, great news," said Braden grumpily. "I get to live life as an incontinent, impotent fool."

"Oh come on. You know the doctor said that would only be temporary.

You're strong as a bull. You'll get through it and be back to normal in no time. We just need to do some research and decide on the best course of treatment – surgery or radiation. If it were me, I'd go for the surgery. Get it cut out. Get rid of it."

"Yeah, I have to admit the thought of going for weeks of radiation therapy isn't appealing to me. At least the surgery will be quicker and hopefully more decisive. But I'll have to take a month or so off work."

"That damn paper can get along fine without you for a while, honey. Your health is much more important to me. I want you around me for a long time."

"Is that right, darlin'? You really mean that? You'll stick around?"

"Of course I will. I'm not going anywhere. I love you and you'll have your own private nurse to take care of you. I'd be willing to move in if you want."

"Yeah? That doesn't sound too bad," said Braden with a smile breaking out. "That doesn't sound too bad at all. I love you too."

He moved toward her. Brought his big beefy arms around her and pulled her slender body tightly against his. He kissed her passionately.

They made love right there on the couch. At least today Braden felt alive again and virile.

He would worry about tomorrow later.

Chapter 26

ST. LUKE'S HOSPITAL

MALCOLM WILKES sat handcuffed in a chair in the lobby of the hospital. Seated next to him were Detective Inspector Peter Moon, a uniformed police officer and Katie Cannon, digital recorder in hand.

Moon tried interrogating the man, but he sat silent. Unresponsive. Defiant.

"Listen, man. Where did you plant the bomb? You're not going anywhere until you tell us. You can keep your ass in that seat until the damn thing goes off."

Beads of sweat broke out on Wilkes's brow. "You'll get blown up too."

"So be it! See you in hell," said Moon angrily. He was determined to break this guy down and get the location of the bomb.

Moon wasn't sure his game of chicken would work so he ordered the uniformed officer to start evacuating people and patients off the third floor where Wilkes had been discovered.

"It's got to be up there on that floor somewhere. Get some other men up there and start searching room by room," he told the police officer. "We'll continue trying to get this motherfucker to talk before we all get our asses blown sky high. Katie, you'd better get out of here now."

"I'm not going anywhere, Peter," she replied defiantly. "This is too big a story."

"Not much good if you don't live to write about it! You can be a stubborn bitch, Katie. I'm ordering you out of this hospital! Now!"

"What are you going to do? Arrest me? I think you've got your hands full as it is. Let me have a talk with your suspect."

Katie turned to Wilkes who was sweating more profusely. "Listen, sir. I'm Katie Cannon of the Daily Express. Do you really want to blow this place up and hurt innocent people? You can be more effective getting your message out through the media. I'd be happy to interview you if you'll just end this drama now."

Wilkes glared at Katie. "I don't want to hurt anybody. I just want the hospital to save that child's life by performing a tracheotomy. They are baby killers!"

"Yes, but how are your actions going to save her? Have you given any thought to the fact that she is still a patient here? I don't know what floor she is on. If you set off that bomb, sir, you could end up killing her yourself. Is that what you really want? Do you really want to be remembered for killing little Emily?"

Wilkes felt as if a hammer hit him. His face showed utter shock. "Oh God, no. I don't want that! I never really thought about that. Please no. I don't want anything to hurt that little girl."

"Then tell us where the bomb is so we can defuse it."

Wilkes hesitated a moment. Then spoke. "It's on the third floor in a briefcase in a storage room."

At that moment, bomb disposal officers arrived at the hospital. Moon relayed where the bomb was located and they headed up to the third floor.

* * *

The two bomb disposal officers studied the open briefcase. The timer was still ticking. 25 minutes....24 minutes...23 minutes....

Three wires, red, green and white went from the timer detonator to the bundle of plastic explosive.

"Which one do we cut?" inquired officer Fred Campell heavily shielded behind a suit of black padding and head visor.

"Damned if I know," replied his similarly garbed colleague Sgt. Bob Harkwell. "But the bomb doesn't appear to be terribly sophisticated."

Harkwell took out some wire cutters and immediately snipped all three wires. "When in doubt, cut em all!"

The timer stopped at 20 minutes. Silence. Officer Campbell breathed a deep sigh of relief.

* * *

Downstairs in the lobby, Moon read Wilkes his rights and took him handcuffed out to a police cruiser. Katie accompanied them taking a statement from Wilkes as they walked.

Then it was off to the Daily Express to file her story:

HOSPITAL BOMBER FOILED.

CHAPTER 27
UNION STATION, TORONTO

AS THE VIA Rail train from Montreal pulled into Union Station, the Scorpion peered out the window into the darkness and bright lights of the city. He saw the CN Tower nearby, brightly lit on its upper deck with red, green and blue lights shimmering. It was an awesome structure. The tower was the focal point of downtown Toronto overlooking the harbor.

The Scorpion and Ali Saleh departed the train into the concourse of Union Station. The Scorpion carried only the brief case. Saleh followed him carrying a suitcase with their clothes. The main concourse had only a sparse gathering of people since it was late at night. 10:10 p.m. according to the large clock overhead.

The two men went out the front entrance and crossed Front Street to the Fairmont Royal York Hotel, situated right across from the train station. The Scorpion went to the front desk and acquired a double-bed room for Saleh and himself to share.

Later in the room, while Saleh watched some television, the Scorpion thought of their mission. Tomorrow they would visit their target and plan their attack.

We are in the heart of the infidels. Operation Saladin will bring death and destruction, as they never before have experienced.

The Scorpion was satisfied their plan was on track.

THE SCORPION

DAY FOUR

WEDNESDAY

CHAPTER 28

HEATHROW AIRPORT, LONDON

TREVOR TREVANIAN and Lynne Whitfield sat in the airport lounge waiting for their early morning Air Canada flight to Toronto.

They arose at 5 a.m. and grabbed a taxi to the airport. After checking their bags and clearing Security, they had some coffee and bacon and eggs at an airport restaurant.

Now they were just waiting for the boarding call, expected in minutes.

"So lover boy, what's this wedding we're attending?" asked Lynne.

"It's my boss, the publisher," replied Trevor. He's getting hitched to another reporter. I understand they've had some kind of secret romance, but it's all out of the closet now."

"How romantic!"

"Well, I received an invitation and it pays to keep in good with the boss. Anyway, it should be fun. The reception is going to be on top of the CN Tower, the world's highest freestanding structure. Ever been to Toronto?"

"Nope. This will be my first visit to Canada. Don't know much about the country, but I do like their men." Lynne playfully punched Trevor in the arm lightly.

"Well, I haven't lived there in a while. I've been stationed overseas for the past five years. But I think I still remember enough about Toronto to show you a good time."

"I'm counting on it. Who knows, maybe I'll catch the bride's bouquet."

"Why. Are you interested in getting married?"

"Not particularly. But you never know, maybe someday the right knight in shining armor will come along."

Trevor grinned. "Well, I'm afraid my armor is a bit tarnished."

Soon the boarding call came for Flight 1220 to Toronto. Trevor and Lynne headed to their plane with the other passengers.

Trevor was now looking forward to this with more anticipation than earlier.

Could be fun and who knows what's in store for us, he thought.

CHAPTER 29
TORONTO DAILY EXPRESS

BRADEN YOUNG was busy in his office looking at the line-up of stories that his reporters were following today:

Donna Marie Pierce was back at the Monica Porter murder trial. The defense was starting its case today and the whole trial was expected to wrap up by Friday.

Katie Cannon would be doing a wrap up piece on the hospital bomber and the latest on the Emily Carter case at St. Luke's Hospital. She was then going on vacation for two weeks for her wedding this Saturday, followed by a honeymoon in Jamaica.

Another new developing story was that of Manuel Talbot, a man who died yesterday from Leukemia while awaiting a stem cell transplant. One had not been found in time and reporter Helen Henderson had been assigned a story on the situation to try to boost public awareness of the donor registry. More than 900 Canadians were seeking a donor and last year only 319 received a stem cell transplant. Less than one percent of the 36 million population were registered in the donor database.

Young had also done some personal online research into prostrate cancer-- its treatments, prognosis and side-effects. Actually he found that the prognosis looked pretty bright if the cancer was caught early.

Leah and he had discussed the various treatments and he was leaning in favor of surgery over the radiation therapy. *Better to get the damn thing cut out and get rid of it. The problem with radiation is always wondering if it will get rid of it and whether it will come back.*

Young had pretty much made up his mind and planned to call the doctors later today to get the ball rolling on setting a surgery date. He would speak to Andrew Chase and take a month's medical leave from the paper.

Anyway, enough of that. Time to get back to the news.

CHAPTER 30

CSIS HEADQUARTERS, OTTAWA

PLENTY OF PAPERWORK was occupying CSIS Director Alexander Cuddy when he was interrupted by a knock on his door.

His deputy director Simon Ward entered the office carrying some documents.

"Boss, you need to see this. We've had some more Intel from our friends at Langley and Homeland Security regarding that terrorist threat. Apparently a female police officer in northern New Hampshire was found off a highway with her throat cut. Her last radio call said she was checking some Arab-looking guys in a Dodge Caravan. The Caravan was later found abandoned in Derby Line, Vermont near the border. It's right next to Stanstead, Quebec."

"Do we think they've crossed over?" inquired Cuddy. "That goddamn place has been a millstone around our necks for far too long. We should have cracked down and put up a security wall years ago, but the damn townspeople on both sides have been fighting it. It's an open invitation for terrorists and smugglers."

"Well sir, we had Border Services check their security camera recordings in Stanstead and it appears five Middle Eastern-looking men crossed individually at varying intervals from the library there. The border bisects it and it is a security-free area. I'm afraid they have crossed into Canada and we don't have a clue as to their final destination."

"Fuckin' hell, Simon!" Cuddy slammed his fist down on his desk. "We need to send out a Red Alert immediately to the RCMP and the provincial and city police forces in Quebec and Ontario. Get those photos and descriptions out right away. We need to track down these fuckers and find out what they're up to. What is this Operation Saladin? And what is their target?"

* * *

Several miles away in another residential area of Ottawa, five men were gathered in a house.

Hashim Hadi, Khaled Kaim and Shareet Halaim had earlier arrived at the safe house in Ottawa where they joined up with two more colleagues, Mohammad Amanijad and Ibrahim Hafiz. Amanijad was a university police officer at the University of Ottawa and Hafiz, a letter carrier with Canada Post.

They had been planted in Ottawa years earlier as part of a secret Al-Qaeda cell. Now they had been activated for their part in Operation Saladin. They would willingly die for the glory of their cause.

The five men sat around a kitchen table drinking coffee. On the table was an armory of weapons, handguns and semi-automatic rifles, along with piles of boxed ammunition.

"Brothers, today we begin our mission of destiny and our journey to Paradise," said Hashim Hadi, the leader of this stage of the Scorpion's operation. "We will not strike today. First we check out the target and devise our strategy. The plan is to hit the infidels on Friday before the Armageddon. We may not be alive to see that happen, but our phase of the operation will cause chaos and confusion in the infidel capital and send a warning and message of destruction to the Great Satan in the south."

The other men nodded their heads in agreement and muttered words of praise.

"Now brothers, let us pray."

The men moved to the living room where five prayer mats lay on the floor. They knelt, facing east towards Mecca, and began to bow and chant their Islamic mantra.

CHAPTER 31

ONTARIO PROVINCIAL COURT #16

JUDGE DEBORAH LIVINGSTONE brought her gavel down sharply. Court was back in session.

"Present your case, Mr. Evans," she told the defense attorney.

Clayton Evans, who was wearing a gray pinstriped suit under his black legal robe, grabbed his lapels as he arose at the defense table. "We call as our first witness, Miss Leslie Porter, your Honor."

A short, thin woman stood from the back seats in the courtroom and made her way to the witness box. She appeared to be in her 20s, wore black glasses and looked like a librarian, very bookish, almost mousey. She was primly dressed in a cream-colored skirt with white blouse.

After she was sworn in the by the Bailiff, Evans approached. "Would you please tell the court your name and who you are?"

"My name is Leslie Porter. I am the daughter of the accused, Mrs. Monica Porter.

At the media table, Donna Marie Pierce busily took notes. She looked closely at the witness. She appeared to be confident and not at all nervous.

THE SCORPION

"Miss Porter. Can you tell this court where you were on Christmas Eve last?"

"Certainly, I was at the house of my parents for Christmas dinner. I was there with my father, mother, and my brother Jeffery and his wife Jeanette."

"So you were present at the dinner table when the incident occurred and your mother shot your father?"

"Yes, I was."

"Please tell the court what happened leading up to the shooting."

Leslie Porter cleared her throat and proceeded calmly. "We had just finished a lovely turkey dinner and were awaiting dessert. The conversation had been mostly pleasant about family matters, what we had all been up to, when my father started talking. Something he said incited some harsh words from my mother."

"What did he say that generated this response from your mother?" inquired Evans.

"I don't really remember," replied Leslie Porter. "Something about his work I think and he mentioned the name of his new lady friend, Gwen. My mother suddenly became agitated and accused him of 'flaunting his slut in her face.' My father became angry and they exchanged some very harsh words. An argument broke out and it was most uncomfortable for us all."

"What happened next?"

"My mother stormed out of the room. We all sat there rather speechless. It felt very uncomfortable and no one knew what to say. She returned within a few minutes, but she was carrying a pistol and she walked up to my father and shot him once in the chest."

"And then what happened, Miss Porter?"

"My mother dropped the gun and started crying. I rushed to assist my father and my brother Jeffery ran to phone 911. The police and paramedics arrived within about 10 minutes. The paramedics began working on my father immediately, trying to resuscitate him, but they said it was too late – he had passed on. The police took my mother into custody and questioned us all about the circumstances."

"I see," said Evans, scratching his chin and starting to pace back and forth in front of the witness box. "Now Miss Porter, how would you describe your mother's state of mind during this incident."

"Objection, your Honor," cried out Crown Attorney Alexander James jumping to his feet. "The witness is not qualified to judge state of mind."

"Not medically perhaps," replied Evans. "But she was a witness to the crime, your Honor and can tell us the demeanor of the accused at the time of the shooting."

"Fair enough, I will allow the witness to answer. Objection overruled," said

THE SCORPION

Judge Livingston. "You may answer the question, Miss Porter."

"Well, I could see she was obviously very distressed. My mother just stood there sobbing. She looked to be in shock and I'm sure she was not herself."

"How had she been in the days preceding this dinner?" asked Evans.

"She had been very depressed over her breakup with my Dad and his fling with that little tart. The doctor had her on several medications for her depression and to help her sleep."

"I see. Thank you very much, Miss Porter."

Judge Livingston then offered Crown Attorney Alexander James a chance to cross-examine the witness.

James approached the witness and stated: "Miss Porter , by your comments I take it you didn't approve of your father's affair with his secretary."

"Certainly not. But men will be men, I suppose. He was still my father and I loved him. I think he was going through a middle age crisis and I only hoped that eventually he would tire of his liaison with that woman and that my parents could work things out and get back together. They had been married for 30 years after all."

"Very impressive. I'm sure you must have been very distressed by this situation. Do you think that deep down you understand why your mother did what she did and that you support her?"

"Obbbbbjection! My learned colleague goes too far, your Honor. This is outrageous." Evans rose to his feet, his face beet red with outrage.

"I have to agree. Your comments are entirely out of line, Mr. James. Withdraw them and rephrase," said Judge Livingstone sternly. If the judge's appearance could freeze, James would be a statue.

"Sorry, your Honor. I apologize and withdraw my remarks. Miss Porter, what do you think of what your mother did?"

"Well, of course I was horrified. I may not have liked what my father did, but I certainly did not want to see him shot and killed over it. I'm sure my mother didn't either, I don't think she knew what she was doing when she pulled that trigger. Maybe it was the drugs or grief, I don't know. But I do know she wasn't in a sane state of mind when she shot my father. She needs help not punishment."

Evans sat smiling at the defense table. This was good stuff. The daughter was a strong witness. He could tell by their reactions that it was having a powerful effect on the jury. James was only helping his case by opening this can of worms.

James began to realize this too and decided to cut his losses and end this harmful testimony.

"That is your opinion, Miss Porter, but you are not a psychologist. Anyway, thank you for your testimony. That will be all."

Judge Livingstone looked at the clock on the wall. 12:05 p.m. "I think it is

THE SCORPION

time to adjourn for lunch. Court will resume at 1:30 with your next witness, Mr. Evans."

The Judge banged her gavel and court adjourned.

CHAPTER 32

DAILY EXPRESS NEWSROOM

U.S. HOSPITAL TAKES BABY EMILY

By Katie Cannon, Staff Writer

Baby Emily is being flown to a hospital in Pittsburgh, Pennsylvania to receive a tracheotomy that will extend her life.

St. Luke's Hospital officials announced today that, at the request of Baby Emily's parents, arrangements have been made to transfer the youngster to Pittsburgh's Three Rivers Hospital.

Emily, 3, suffers from a severe neurological disorder that has left her in a vegetative state and St. Luke's doctors have refused to perform a tracheotomy. The hospital applied to the province's Consent and Capacity Board to remove her breathing tube and allow nature to take its course in the best interests of the child and to alleviate further suffering. Permission to remove the tube was granted by the CCB to allow Emily to die.

Emily's parents opposed the decision and hired lawyer Brian Bakker who received a court injunction to stop the procedure pending a legal review of the

THE SCORPION

case.

The case has sparked widespread controversy on both sides of the border, with various Right to Life and religious groups coming to the support of Baby Emily.

Police yesterday foiled a recent bomb attempt at St. Luke's. Malcolm Wilkes, 46, of Toronto, has been charged in connection with the incident.

Benjamin Moore, chairman of the hospital board, said that the hospital in cooperation with the family and legal representatives of Baby Emily have arranged with Three Rivers Hospital in Pittsburgh to perform the procedure.

"Our sympathies go out to the family in this tragic situation," said Moore. "Our position in this matter was taken by our top medical experts in what we consider the best interests of the child to alleviate further suffering."

But Moore said continuing discussions with the family led to finding a hospital in the U.S. that has agreed to perform the surgical procedure to extend Emily's life. Pro-life groups have raised money to support the family and the costs of the operation in Pittsburgh.

Following the procedure, Emily will be sent home to live out her remaining days with her parents.

Brian Bakker, legal representative for the family, said: "We are very pleased that the hospital has acceded to the family's request. We thank Three Rivers

Hospital in Pittsburgh for agreeing to perform the procedure and giving little Emily a chance to spend more time with her family. We also thank the many groups that have supported her cause both financially and with words of encouragement. Emily's family is most appreciative."

A legal fund has been established to help the family with out of country medical expenses that are not covered under the provincial health plan. Donations may be made to the Baby Emily Fund at any branch of the Royal Bank of Canada.

Katie Cannon checked over her copy and typed the traditional – 30 -- at the bottom of the page signifying The End.

She felt satisfied with her story and pushed the key on the computer, sending it to the Final Copy folder where editors would later look at it and make their editing changes.

She left her desk and walked over to Braden Young's office. After rapping on the door, she entered. Young was busy editing something on his computer screen.

"Katie, come on in'" he said exuberantly. "Getting excited about the wedding? Not long now."

"No, it's coming up soon and we've still got some last minute details to take care of," said Katie. "Just wanted you to know, Boss, that my final story in the

Baby Emily case is done and ready to go."

"Great, Katie. You've done a fine job and I want to thank you for the extra effort. I know it has not been easy what with the wedding preparations and all. You're a real trooper and this paper is all the better for having such a great reporter."

"Well, I'm off on vacation now for two weeks. Andrew and I still have many details to finalize with the wedding and then we're off to Jamaica for our honeymoon."

"You deserve the break, kid. I hope things go well for you on Saturday."

"You and Leah will be coming, right?"

"Of course, we wouldn't miss it for the world. Leah's really looking forward to it and dining at the top of the CN Tower."

"Yes, it should be quite the experience for everybody. Well, see you later, Braden."

Katie departed Young's office feeling on top of the world. She'd finished her story and now only looked forward to the joy of her wedding day. After all, she was getting married to her soulmate and the love of her life, followed by 10 days in Jamaica with sun, sand and sex.

Could life be any better?

CHAPTER 33

DOWNTOWN TORONTO

THE SCORPION left the hotel and walked quickly toward the target.

He told Ali Saleh to stay in the room until he returned. If Saleh got hungry, order room service, he instructed. Under no circumstances was he to leave the room.

After several minutes on the busy Toronto streets, the Scorpion arrived at the main entrance to the target through its famous enclosed Skywalk from York Street. The CN Tower is located two blocks from Union Station, adjacent to the Rogers Centre where the American League Toronto Blue Jays and NBA Toronto Raptors play.

The Scorpion gazed skywards up to the top of the tower and its revolving dome. Impressive. The CN Tower is the world's tallest tower, standing 1,815 feet above the Toronto skyline and is one of Canada's most recognizable and celebrated icons.

The perfect launch pad for their Armageddon, the Scorpion thought. The small nuke would detonate and obliterate the tower, spreading radiation over the city and if the winds were right, the radiation would drift over Lake Ontario and hit

THE SCORPION

Niagara Falls and Buffalo, New York. Thousands, if not millions, would get sick and die of radiation poisoning. *Just retribution for the infidels.*

The Scorpion entered the tower's main lobby. It was a busy place with thousands of people bustling about in the various shops, cafés and entertainment facilities. They were some of the more than two million people who visit the tower each year.

He headed to a nearby ticket kiosk and purchased a ticket to ride the high-speed elevators to the Lookout Level, the viewing point atop the structure.

He shot to the top in only 58 seconds, seeing the ground disappear below him as he ascended through the glass-fronted wall of the elevator. He felt his ears pop as the pressure built during the ascent.

At the top, he got a marvelous view of the city and the lake. It was a sunny, cloudless day and the view was magnificent. There was a slight reticence that such a magnificent structure had to be destroyed. But it was a symbol of the decadence and profanity of the infidel world. Just like the World Trade Towers in New York. Their towers and accoutrements of power and injustice must crumble and shatter into dust for all eternity.

The Scorpion spent a few minutes walking around the viewing pod. Then he went down to another level where the glass floor was situated. He felt strange as walked on it looking down at the people, like tiny ants, scurrying along the streets below. They had no idea what awaited them.

He then took the elevator down to another floor where the 360 Restaurant was located. The restaurant is 1,151 feet above ground and revolves a complete circle every 72 minutes to give diners a spectacular view of the city.

As he came off the elevator, a Maître D' confronted the Scorpion.

"Good afternoon, sir. Will it be one for lunch today?" he asked.

"No, I'm afraid not. I'm just checking the place out," replied the Scorpion. "We're visitors to your fine city and a friend and I were thinking of having dinner here Saturday night. Will we need reservations?"

"Usually yes. But I'm afraid that won't be possible this Saturday. The restaurant is reserved for a private party – a wedding reception."

"Oh, what a wonderful place for a wedding reception," the Scorpion enthused. "It must be someone pretty important and wealthy to afford to hire the whole place out."

"Most certainly," replied the Maître D' excitedly. "It is Mr. Andrew Chase, the publisher of the Daily Express. He's getting married and it will be the society event of the year. Many important people will be here, including the Mayor and numerous high ranking officials in the federal and provincial governments."

"Really? That is impressive. I'm sure you're all excited to be hosting such an event. There must be a lot of preparation involved."

THE SCORPION

"There certainly is. All our staff will be very busy and we have hired additional temporary staff. There will be almost 400 people attending this reception."

"Well, I wish you well and hope everything goes according to plan. I hope you have a memorable experience. I'll talk things over with my friend and perhaps we'll plan dinner for another time. We're in the city for a few days."

"Fine, sir. Just call our reservation line. Have a nice day!"

"You too," said the Scorpion with a warm smile. "And thanks for the information. You've been most helpful."

Indeed he had. This would be the perfect setting for their bomb. Not only would it take out the tower, but also half the elite of Toronto society.

Allah be praised.

CHAPTER 34

ONTARIO PROVINCIAL COURT #16

THE MURDER TRIAL resumed for its afternoon session.

Judge Deborah Livingston fidgeted on the bench as the lawyers prepared to begin their arguments. Donna Marie Pierce settled herself at the media table and pulled out her notebook, pen and digital micro-recorder. She was feeling a little tipsy.

I shouldn't have had that second glass of Merlot at lunch, she thought.

"The defense wishes to call Jeffery Porter," said Clayton Evans, the defense attorney.

The Bailiff called out Jeffery Porter's name. A portly man with thick, silver hair made his way to the witness box.

"State your name and affiliation to the deceased, please," said Evans in a matter of fact fashion. This part of trials was routine and meant to get the witness on the official record.

"My name is Jeffery Porter and I am the son of Malcolm Porter."

"And what is your occupation, sir?"

"I am an investment banker with the Bank of Montreal in Toronto."

"You were at the dinner the night your father was shot?"

"I was. I attended with my wife Jeannette."

"Would you tell the court what transpired at this dinner, please."

Jeffery paused a moment to clear his throat before continuing. "As my sister Leslie testified earlier, we had just finished a lovely dinner and were awaiting dessert when a heated argument broke out between my mother and father. She left the room and returned a few minutes later. She was carrying my father's service pistol and fired a single shot into his chest. Leslie went to the aid of my father and I called 911 for police and an ambulance.

"And how would you describe your mother's mood and actions?"

"Completely irrational. She stood there sobbing and was in a total state of shock."

"I see. And how would your describe your mother's state of mind leading up to these events?"

"Very fragile. She has been seeing a doctor and has been on anti-depressant medications and sleep aids for some weeks. She has been very distraught the past few weeks over the breakup with my father."

"Thank you, Mr. Porter. That's all the questions I have."

"Mr. James, your witness," declared Judge Livingston.

"No questions, your Honor." Crown Attorney James decided to leave things alone after the session with Leslie Porter, which might have caused some harm to his case. *Let sleeping dogs lie.*

Evans then arose from his seat. "The defense next would like to call Dr. David Johns," he said.

Johns, a slender, wiry middle-aged man, who wore a bow tie, took his seat in the witness box.

After the necessary introductions, he stated that he was Mrs. Porter's doctor. Upon prompting from the defense attorney, he told the court he had been treating her for acute depression, anxiety and sleep disorder.

"And what medications was she on?" inquired Evans.

"Prozac for the depression and Lorazepam for the anxiety and sleep disorder," replied Johns.

"Please tell us a bit about these drugs and what they do."

"Prozac is used to treat severe cases of depression. Mrs. Porter was receiving 20 mg. She was having severe depression over her marital difficulties. Lorazepam is used for treatment of anxiety and insomnia. Mrs. Porter said she was having great difficulty sleeping and she was prone to frequent weeping."

"I see. But doctor, isn't it also true that these drugs can have some serious side effects?"

"In some cases, yes. All drugs have side effects. It's often a matter of weighing whether the benefits outweigh the risks. In the case of depression, Prozac can be very effective in controlling this. We also monitor our patients closely."

Evans paced in front of Johns before posing his next question. "But doctor, isn't it true that there have been cases of some patients developing psychotic episodes from the use of Prozac? I have read of cases where patients on Prozac have committed suicide or harmed others."

Johns nodded his head in agreement. "Yes, one of the serious side effects can be suicidal or agitated behavior."

"Thank you, Dr. Johns. No further questions." Evans smiled. He got the answer he wanted and saw the reaction on the faces of the jury.

Judge Livingston invited Alexander James to cross examine.

"Dr. Evans, these so-called side effects are rare, aren't they?" asked James.

"Well, not exactly rare, but they are miniscule. They don't crop up often, but they do affect some patients with psychotic behavior."

"But you have been monitoring, Mrs. Porter, haven't you? Have you seen any indications of psychotic behavior?"

"Well, I had seen her weekly for the month prior to the incident. She did not report any adverse effects or exhibit any symptoms to me, but I cannot swear that she was not experiencing them. She may have experienced a psychotic break under undue stress."

"But you also cannot positively swear that she experienced such a psychotic break and effects from the drugs, can you, doctor?"

"No."

"Thank you, Dr. Evans. The Crown is finished with this witness."

Judge Livingstone turned to Clayton Evans. "Mr. Evans, does the defense have any further witnesses to call?"

Evans had contemplated putting Monica Porter on the stand, but rejected the idea as too risky. He didn't want to put further stress on her and subject her to cross-examination by the Crown. He felt he had made his case and created reasonable doubt as to her sanity.

"No, your Honor. The defense rests," he stated.

"Fine. Since it's now almost 4 p.m., we will adjourn for today and have final summations in the morning at 9 a.m.," said the Judge, bringing down her gavel once again to close proceedings.

CHAPTER 35

24 SUSSEX DRIVE, OTTAWA

THE FORD ESCAPE drove along the quiet residential streets of the New Edinburgh neighborhood in Ottawa. It is an area of large historic, residential homes, many made of limestone. Many of the buildings were foreign embassies.

Inside the vehicle were five men -- Hashim Hadi, Khaled Kaim, Shareet Halaim, Ibrahim Hafiz and Mohammad Amanijad. Hadi was driving.

As the vehicle wound along Sussex Drive, it passed the French Embassy with the Ottawa River behind it. The vehicle came to a stop outside #24, just across the road from Rideau Hall, the large official residence of the Governor General of Canada.

Behind the iron gates and fence sat a large limestone structure. This is the official residence of the Prime Minister of Canada.

Unlike 10 Downing Street or the White House, it is used almost exclusively as a place of residence for the Prime Minister and his family and for occasional receptions. The PM's work is carried out in offices in the Langevin Block, near Parliament Hill.

Hadi told the others to stay put, while he and Khaled Kaim got out of the

SUV.

He stood at the entranceway and started shooting photos with a small, digital camera. The imposing house stood in the background, to the right was a guardhouse with several Royal Canadian Mounted Police officers inside. Hadi viewed one policeman patrolling the grounds.

Security was overhauled at 24 Sussex Drive following a November 1995 attempted assassination by André Dallaire who wandered around the house and grounds for nearly an hour before being confronted outside Prime Minister Jean Chrétien's bedroom by his wife Aline. She locked the door to the bedroom, while Chrétien guarded his wife and himself with an Inuit stone carving. Ultimately RCMP officers arrested Dallaire before anyone got hurt.

Measures to boost security were taken after this incident, adding several more guards to the property, the installation of crash-proof barriers within the main gates and the addition of several more security cameras for the house and grounds.

One of the police officers came out of the guardhouse and strolled over to the entranceway.

"Sorry, sir. You'll have to move off. This is restricted, private property," he said politely. The officers were used to tourists stopping at the entrance to grab a few photos.

"Oh, officer. We're just visitors to your fine city. We just wanted a photo of your Prime Minister's house," said a smiling and gracious Hadi.

"Fine, get your photo and off you go," replied the Mountie in his traditional red serge ceremonial uniform.

"Would you mind?" Hadi handed the camera to Kaim and stood next to the Mountie.

Always accommodating to tourists, the Mountie allowed Kaim to take the photo.

"Okay, now off you go my fine chap and enjoy your visit to our national capital." The Mountie waved them to move along.

"Oh, we will," said Hadi as the two men returned to the SUV. "I'm sure this will be a most memorable trip."

It will also be one the infidels never forget, Hadi thought as he entered the Escape.

CHAPTER 36

PEARSON INTERNATIONAL AIRPORT

TREVOR TREVANIAN and Lynne Whitfield made their way easily through Customs and Immigration and waited at the carousel for their bags.

They made their way through the terminal to Ground Transportation. Trevanian knew there were buses to the various downtown hotels, but he didn't want to wait after the long flight, so he hailed a cab.

Forty-five minutes later they were ensconced in their room in the Westin Harbor Castle overlooking Lake Ontario. It was early evening and the sun was starting to sink over the blue horizon.

Lynne lay on the bed and pulled Trevor gently towards her.

"Tired?" he asked.

"Never too tired for you," she replied with a smile.

Trevor wrapped his body over hers and kissed her passionately, first on her cherry red lips and then on her slender neck. He was bone-tired after the long transatlantic flight, but felt the stirring in his loins.

"Hungry for dinner yet?" he inquired.

"Maybe later. Let's have dessert first."

So they did.

JAMES A. ANDERSON

DAY FIVE

THURSDAY

CHAPTER 37

TORONTO DAILY EXPRESS

BRADEN YOUNG edited copy on his computer terminal while sipping a Tim Hortons extra large, double-double coffee.

Suddenly his phone rang and he answered.

"Mr. Young, Dr. Bock here. I just wanted to let you know that we have your prostate surgery booked for September 1. There's a bit of a backlog, but we had a cancellation so I've squeezed you in then. Hope that meets your approval."

"Fine, Doc. That'll be great." Braden had a lump in his throat and found it difficult to breathe. Anxiety. He'd hoped to get the surgery over with as soon as possible. But this would allow him the summer to get his affairs in order…..just in case! He also wanted to take Leah on some exotic vacation before he went under the knife and the protracted recovery.

"Good," replied Dr. Bock. "Then we'll have you check into the hospital the night before. And don't worry about this, Mr. Young. You're going to be fine. We have an exceptionally high success rate with these early stage cancers."

"Thank you, doctor." Braden hung up the phone. *Yeah, don't worry! It's not you having your nuts cut up.*

* * *

Later that morning over in Provincial Court #16, the Porter trial resumed and the attorneys were making their final summations.

Crown Attorney Alexander James walked in a criss-cross pattern in front of the jurors as he made his address.

"Ladies and gentlemen of the jury, you have a huge decision before you today. There is no doubt here that Mrs. Porter fatally shot her husband Malcolm last Christmas Eve. What you have to decide is whether that was a deliberate act or the act of an irrational, temporarily insane woman in danger of losing her husband to another woman.

"I think we have presented sufficient evidence during the course of this trial to prove that Mrs. Monica Porter knew exactly what she was doing that day. In the aftermath of a heated argument, she coldly walked away from the room, retrieved Mr. Porter's service pistol and returned to the dining room to fatally shoot him with it in front of his family.

"While we can sympathize with Mrs. Porter over the anguish of the break-up of her marriage, murder must not go unpunished. Members of the jury, it is your responsibility today to send that message to society and return a verdict of GUILTY."

With his summation concluded, James returned to his seat satisfied that he had done his best and made a solid case.

THE SCORPION

The judge then asked defense attorney Clayton Evans to make his final argument.

"Thank you, your Honor," said Evans grasping the lapels of his robe as he addressed the jury. "Ladies and gentlemen of the jury, my learned colleague is correct when he states that there is no doubt here today that my client did indeed shoot her husband.

"But what we have to ask ourselves is WHY? Why does a respectable mother and wife, a prominent member of society who contributes to many charities and social causes, suddenly pick up a gun and shoot her husband?

"There is no doubt that Mrs. Porter was a woman in distress and not of sane mind when she committed this unfortunate act. You have heard testimony from her children about the extreme anxiety, distress and suffering she was undergoing due to the break-up of her long marriage and her husband's unfortunate dalliance with a younger woman.

"You have heard testimony from her doctor as to her state of mind. That she was taking drugs, drugs that are known to have possible side effects in some cases. Drugs that can cause a psychotic break or irrational act to harm herself or others. I submit to you that this is the case here. Mrs. Monica Porter didn't know what she was doing when she pulled that trigger.

"She suffers extreme remorse at her actions and the loss of her husband and life partner by her own hand. I submit to you, ladies and gentlemen of the jury, that this is a classic case of temporary insanity, fuelled by high anxiety and a reaction to drugs."

Evans looked at the jury and saw from their faces that his comments were drawing a reaction, especially from the women jurors who could relate to Mrs. Porter's circumstances. Now was the time to drive home his central point.

"Ladies and gentlemen, you do have a big decision here today. To either send Mrs. Porter to prison to pay for this crime or to find her NOT GUILTY by reason of insanity and send her to a psychiatric clinic for needed treatment. What is in the best long-term interests of society? That decision is yours. I hope you choose wisely. Thank you."

"Thank you, Mr.Evans. I think that concludes this trial," said Judge Deborah Livingston. She turned to the jury and began giving them final instructions on their deliberations, which were about to begin.

"You basically have two things to consider here," said the Judge solemnly. "Either you return a verdict of guilty of murder in the second degree or not guilty by reason of insanity. Please consider the evidence carefully and God help you in your task."

She asked the Bailiff to lead the jury to a room where they would discuss the evidence, debate it and make their decision on the fate of Monica Porter.

CHAPTER 38

DOWNTOWN TORONTO

AFTER GRABBING an early breakfast at the hotel coffee shop, Trevor Trevanian and Lynne Whitfield set out to do some sightseeing and shopping.

Trevor was anxious to show Lynne some of the sights of Toronto. They visited the Hockey Hall of Fame where Lynne got to see the Stanley Cup in its display case. Trevor was a big Maple Leafs fan, but sadly it had been many years since they last had their names carved on the famous silver trophy donated by Lord Stanley, a former Governor General of Canada, in 1892.

They visited the national headquarters of the Canadian Broadcasting Corporation, one of three national TV networks in the country. The taxpayer subsidizes this public broadcaster, while the other two networks CTV and Global are privately run.

As they left the CBC after taking the public tour of the facilities, Trevor said: "Now hon, I know you'd love to do some shopping and we'll go to the Eaton Centre right after I drop by the paper. I should let them know I'm in town. My visit should only take a few minutes. We can check out some of the shops along Yonge Street. It's one of the longest streets in the world, running north forever out of Toronto."

"Shopping. Music to a gal's ears," said Lynne smiling warmly. "That's OK Trev, take all the time you need at the paper. But I need to find a decent dress for this wedding. You don't want me wearing the tatty old things I brought with me."

"Listen, you'll be the best looking one there, with the exception of the bride," teased Trevor.

They headed over to Dundas Street and the Daily Express building.

* * *

"Trevor, my man. Wonderful to see you," said Braden Young as Trevor and Lynne entered his office.

"Braden, you old son of a bitch, how's it hanging?"

"Same old stuff, you know the newspaper game. So you decided to come back for the boss's wedding, eh."

"Yup. And I brought some company. Braden, this is my date, Lynne Whitfield – she's a journalist in England."

Braden stood up and shook hands with Lynne. "Nice to meet you, Lynne. Welcome to Canada. Although why you'd want to come with this reprobate baffles me."

"Well, I thought he needed some class, especially at a high society wedding like this one."

Braden grinned. "You got that right. But he's one hell of a journalist and his interview with Osama bin Laden probably saved this paper's bacon. I'm getting too damn old to go hunting for a new job. And I rather like this one."

"The Daily Express wouldn't be the same without you at the helm, Braden," said Trevor seriously for a change.

"How's the new gig going? Settled in London all right?"

"Well, it's nice to be back in civilization after Afghanistan. MI-6 even hauled me in a few days ago. They were trying to recruit me as a spy. They think I'm still in contact with Al-Qaeda and can help them out."

"Whoaaaa! Stay well away from those spooks. You don't want them getting their hooks into you.

"I have no intention of getting into bed with them. Don't worry, Braden."

Lynne just stood there smiling and silent.

CHAPTER 39

COWBOYS BAR & GRILL

COWBOYS WAS DOING a booming pre-lunch business. The country and western-themed bar, situated just down the street from the courthouse, was filled with people, including lawyers and media people from the trial awaiting the jury's verdict in the Porter murder trial.

"Any idea how long we will have to wait?" inquired Donna-Marie Pierce to defense lawyer Clayton Evans. She sat down at his table with his team of lawyers, hoping to get a short interview.

"Your guess is as good as mine, young lady," replied Evans. "It could be a few hours or a few days. Generally, the longer it goes is usually better for us since it means the jury is deadlocked. A quick verdict usually means guilty, although not all the time. The OJ Simpson case is a classic example."

"Well, Mr.Evans, on the record, how do you think you did?"

"I'm pleased with our case and our position. I believe we made a strong case for temporary insanity. We've done all we can. Now it's in the hands of 12 good citizens."

Pierce asked several more questions and received stock media responses

THE SCORPION

from Evans. He was used to the media limelight and came up with glib answers easily.

Donna Marie silently hoped to herself that the trial didn't drag on too long. She was supposed to be a bridesmaid at Katie Cannon's wedding and the rehearsal was Friday evening. Surely, there would be a verdict before then. And she still had the story to write for the paper.

* * *

Across town at Andrew's condo, Katie and Andrew were getting ready to do some last minute wedding preparations. There still seemed hundreds of small things to do and time was getting short.

Katie was feeling a little anxious with all the pressure. Strange. As a journalist she should be used to deadline pressure. But this was different. This was her dream wedding to her dream prince. And she wanted everything to be perfect.

"So, hon, what's first on the agenda," said Andrew who didn't seem a bit fazed by the preparations.

"Well sweetie, we need to go to the jeweler's to pick up the rings. We also need to pick up the gifts for the best man and bridesmaids. I thought we could check out what the jewelry store has to offer."

"Great idea," said Andrew. "One–stop shopping. You know me – get in, get what you want and get out!"

"Just like most men," Katie smiled.

* * *

At Nash Jewelry, Katie Cannon and Andrew Chase were picking up their wedding rings.

"They are ready for you," said Samuel Nash, the owner. He held out two ring boxes with their lids open.

Katie sucked in her breath as she gazed on hers. It was a stunning gold band with three half-carat diamonds. "It's amazing!"

"And inscribed just as you wanted it, Mr. Chase: *To Katie, with my eternal love. Andrew.*"

Andrew picked up his ring, a plain gold band. He read the simple inscription inside: *06/23/12. Love always, Katie.*"

"Just wanted to make sure you never forget our anniversary," said a grinning Katie.

Andrew kissed her gently on the lips. "Never in a million years!"

Nash then started showing them various trinkets for possible gifts to the wedding party. They eventually opted for silver goblets for the men inscribed: *Thanks for being part of our special day. Katie and Andrew.* The gift for the women was a small gold bracelet with the same inscription.

Andrew pulled out his American Express Platinum card to pay for the items and thanked Nash.

"No, I thank you, Mr. Young. It has been my pleasure to be of assistance. I wish you both a long and happy life together."

As Katie and Andrew left the store, they hugged. They both felt on top of the world.

"When are your parents coming, hon?" asked Andrew.

"They're driving down from Hamilton tomorrow and planning to stay at the Royal York Hotel."

Katie felt a little sad for Andrew because he wouldn't have any family there on his special day. His parents were dead and he had no brothers or sisters. His Best Man was going to be Paul Mann, a college buddy from his University of Toronto days. Mann worked as an editor for the Calgary Herald and was flying in Friday to attend the wedding.

Despite his power and influence, Andrew was something of a loner, with not many close friends. His work was his life, so his side of the guest list included many of the people at the newspaper he worked with and people in politics and the business world. Life could be lonely at the top. But Andrew wasn't complaining. He was about to marry his soulmate, best friend and one of the most beautiful, smart and feisty women in the world.

***

At the Royal York Hotel, the Scorpion and Ali Saleh were back in their room. They had left earlier for some food in the coffee shop.

"We will strike the tower Saturday night, Ali," said the Scorpion. "There is a big wedding with lots of socialites attending and powerful people. It will send a strong message to the infidels that the arm of Islam is long and retribution will be ours. We will be able to blend in with the workers to carry out our mission. It is a perfect opportunity."

The Scorpion walked over to the briefcase in a corner and set it out on the bed. He pulled out a sheet of instructions.

Now Ali, you must familiarize yourself with this device. You will be able to trigger it manually or by a timer. When the time is right, you must allow me time to put some distance from the tower. I will be going to the airport. You have been chosen to carry out this high honor. It will be your ticket to Paradise my friend. I wish I could join you, but I am needed elsewhere to carry on the fight against the infidels."

Damn right. The Scorpion had no intention of immolating himself in the nuclear explosion. That was for the poor sheep like Ali who had been brainwashed into the glory of Islam and thoughts of a gateway to Paradise and umpteen virgins. Fools that they were. But they were useful to the cause, just as those who strapped on bombs and sacrificed themselves for Allah.

THE SCORPION

Combined with the mission in Ottawa, Operation Saladin would go down in the annals of history.

The Scorpion was the mastermind. He would ensure his place in the pantheon of great conquerors like Genghis Khan, Alexander the Great, Napoleon, Adolf Hitler and Tamarlane, a devout Muslim and prodigious killer who had never lost a battle.

That thought was most pleasing to the Scorpion.

CHAPTER 40

AL-QAEDA SAFE HOUSE, OTTAWA

THE FIVE AL-QAEDA operatives in the safe house busied themselves cleaning their weapons.

On the table was an armory of weapons: handguns, machine guns and semi-automatic rifles, along with boxes of ammunition. It was quite an arsenal – Uzis, 9 MM Glock 17s, and AR-15A3s, AK-47s plus some hand grenades. Most of it had been purchased from the Russians who would sell to anyone on the black market.

Hashim Hadi, Khaled Kaim, Shareet Halaim, Mohammad Amanijad and Ibrahim Hafiz were all devout Muslims. They were all products of the Al-Qaeda training camps and had served in Afghanistan, Pakistan and Yemen. They had carried out terrorist acts in Rome, Athens and London.

This was their first foray into North America and the heart of the Great Satan and its allies. They knew they likely would not survive this mission. But so be it. They would advance proudly to Paradise and be remembered here on Earth as Heroes of Islam.

Hashim took out a long scimitar. He began to polish the blade until it gleamed. Soon enough it would be stained with blood. The blood of the Prime Minister of Canada.

THE SCORPION

They planned to assassinate him tomorrow night and behead him as a symbol to the other infidel leaders of the ultimate fate that awaited them.

CHAPTER 41

COWBOYS BAR & GRILL

TIM MCGRAW'S "Live Like You Were Dying" blared out through the noisy bar as people drank and talked.

The lunch hour rush had passed, but the bar was still busy – packed with lawyers, journalists and onlookers from the Porter trial down the street. It was 2:25 p.m.

Clayton Evans held court at his table with his party of lawyers and assistants, regaling them with stories from his many cases as he sipped on a Heineken.

Donna Marie Pierce sat quietly listening with her gin and tonic in hand.

What a pompous jerk! But he's an excellent lawyer. I'd definitely want him if my ass was in a sling, legally speaking.

Suddenly Evans was interrupted by his cell phone ringing. He picked up the phone and listened for a few seconds, a slight frown coming to his forehead.

"LADIES AND GENTLEMEN!" he shouted above the barroom din. "The jury's back. We have a verdict! Time to go." Dropping his voice to a low whisper, he added: "It's just been three hours. Don't know whether that's good or bad, but I guess we're about to find out."

Like a herd of elephants, everyone stormed out of the bar.

* * *

Judge Deborah Livingston convened the court.

Everyone took their places. The lawyers sat at their respective tables, the journalists at the media table and the 12-person jury sitting solemnly in the box.

Donna Marie gazed over at the jurors, trying to read their faces. It was an impossible task trying to read them. They just sat stone-faced.

"Members of the jury, have you reached a verdict?" asked Judge Livingston.

A middle-aged woman with streaks of grey in her black hair stood. "We have, your Honor."

"And is it unanimous?"

"It is."

"Fine." The judge beckoned to the Bailiff who retrieved a piece of white paper from the Foreperson of the jury panel. He walked it over to the judge who glanced at it briefly. Her face did not show any emotion.

"Members of the jury, how do you find in the case of the Crown versus Monica Porter?" she asked.

"We find the defendant NOT GUILTY of murder in the second degree by reason of insanity," replied the matronly juror.

A gasp echoed through the courtroom. Clayton Evans turned in triumph to his client and hugged Monica Porter, gently patting her on the back. The prosecution lawyers had a resigned look of defeat on their faces.

"Thank you for your great service and your thoughtful deliberations," Judge Livingston told the jury. "Would the defendant please rise."

In accordance with the law, the judge now had to pass sentence. Monica Porter had been found not guilty, but she could not go free. Because of the insanity finding, she needed psychiatric treatment.

"Monica Porter, a jury of your peers has found you not guilty by reason of insanity. It is the decision of this court to remand you to the Clarke Institute of Psychiatry for an indefinite period to receive psychiatric treatment. It will be up to the doctors there to determine when that treatment is successful and to release you at a later date."

Clayton Evans was satisfied. He'd won the case and spared his client a lengthy prison term. It was the best possible outcome given the circumstances. Evans knew the Clarke Institute's reputation for high quality psychiatric evaluation and care. Monica would be treated and probably be released within a year or so to return to her life and family. Although things for her would probably never be quite the same.

Donna Marie Pierce left the courtroom quickly. She had a story to file.

THE SCORPION

DAY SIX

FRIDAY

CHAPTER 42

CSIS HEADQUARTERS, OTTAWA

"ANY WORD YET on these terrorists, Simon?" inquired CSIS Director Alexander Cuddy who was already on his fourth cup of coffee at 10 a.m.

"Nothing," said his deputy director Simon Ward. "It's like they don't exist." Ward was fidgety and nervous.

"Oh, they exist alright. And they're up to something. Why can't we get any fucking Intel on these motherfuckers?"

"Well, they're obviously lying low," said Ward cautiously, not wanting to piss off his boss any further. "If they're not moving about, it's hard for us to get a fix on them. They must be holed up somewhere planning something."

"Yes, but what? This is a huge country they could be anywhere by now and we're helpless until they make a move on this goddamn Operation Saladin."

Cuddy slammed his cup down the desk, spilling coffee over some papers spread on top. "Shit!"

* * *

The five terrorists were at prayer in a house only three miles away from

Cuddy.

They were about to embark on their mission and none of them expected to return. They expected to reunite in Paradise.

As they finished their prayers and arose from the mats on the floor, they picked them up and stored them in a cupboard. They began to gather their cashload of weapons. Hashim Hadi picked up the scimitar and carried it in its sheath along with an Uzi.

"It is time, brothers," said Hadi. "We must launch our mission and teach the infidels a lesson. May Allah be with us!"

CHAPTER 43

HY'S STEAK HOUSE, TORONTO

KATIE CANNON, her fiancé Andrew Chase and his Best Man Paul Mann were eating lunch at this famous steakhouse on Bloor Street.

Paul had flown in from Calgary that morning and met them at the restaurant. He was fortyish, tall and thin with a Paul Newman-like smile.

"So this is the young lady who finally snagged you," quipped Paul . "You never told me she was so beautiful. What on earth do you see in this rake, Katie?"

"You're one to talk. Paul was the biggest ladies man at U of T. I was surprised he ever got the time to write for the student paper," said Andrew with a grin.

"So you guys met at university on The Varsity?" inquired Katie.

"We did," replied Paul. "Andrew was the managing editor and I was one of his scribes."

"Hack ....more like it. He was an okay writer, but couldn't spell worth a damn. I was constantly fixing up his errors. One day I threw him a dictionary and told him to use it once in a while. So how are things at the Herald, Paul? I heard they finally made you an editor."

"Yup. City Editor. Now I get to fix up the copy of my young reporters."

"Now that's the blind leading the blind!" Paul and Andrew both laughed. "Get fixed up at your hotel, OK?"

"Oh yes," said Paul. "I'm over at the Westin. I always stay at a Westin when I travel – love their beds. So everything ready for the big day?"

"Pretty much," replied Katie. "The rehearsal is at the church tonight at 6 and we're having a small reception for the wedding party afterwards at Wayne Gretzky's.

"Good. Glad for you both. Seriously Katie, I think you will be good for this guy – perhaps you'll keep him on an even keel."

"No doubt about that," stated Andrew.

The trio continued to talk and reminisce over their meal and some Cabernet. Katie was impressed at the close friendship of the two men as they recalled their student days.

* * *

Over at the Daily Express, Braden Young sat at his desk munching on a tuna salad sandwich and checking the front page of today's paper. It was a very satisfying news day.

NOT GUILTY VERDICT

By Donna Marie Pierce

THE SCORPION

The 60-point bold headline screamed across the top of the page with Pierce's story about the conclusion of the Monica Porter murder trial.

Below it were two other headlines and stories:

REPUBLICAN CANDIDATES RIP INTO OBAMA

President's veto of oil pipeline from Canada criticized

SYRIAN ARMY KILLS THOUSANDS OF PROTESTERS

Young was pleased at today's paper. It had a good range of stories that should captivate reader interest. Now it was on to prepare Saturday's paper, always the largest of the week. It was also going to be Katie and Andrew's wedding day. Quite a big day indeed!

Braden wondered: *What would the rest of today bring?*

CHAPTER 44

24 SUSSEX DRIVE, OTTAWA

PRIME MINISTER Roger Hooper sat at the kitchen table with his wife Sylvia and their two children Mark and Sasha. They were eating Kraft Dinner, a favorite of the two kids, aged 8 and 6 respectively.

Since it was summer, Parliament was not in session and Hooper decided to take the day off from his office duties to spend it with his family. Political life was harsh and meant he had to spend a lot of time away from them. He tried to give the children as normal a life as possible, living in the fishbowl of the public eye.

Hooper was a handsome man of 55. He possessed a shock of silver hair, immaculately groomed at the parliamentary barber shop. He'd put on a few pounds with all the receptions he was forced to attend and the unhealthy, calorie-packed snacks they served. His wife Sylvia was 50 and a stunning brunette for a middle-aged woman. She had a high forehead and Grecian-style nose, a product of her Greek background.

She and Roger had met in college in Alberta at the University of Alberta in Edmonton. Roger had been a star football quarterback and Sylvia a cheerleader.

Their romance blossomed and after graduation they married. When Roger entered the political arena in local politics, Sylvia was a definite asset as a political wife and stood by him as his political star ascended.

He became a city councillor, later jumped into federal politics as a Member of Parliament and four years ago was elected leader of the Progressive Conservative Party. Hooper led them to a majority government in the next election. He was still popular in the polls.

"So, my dear what's on the agenda today?" asked Sylvia.

"Well, I have some paperwork to take care of this afternoon and we're scheduled to attend a reception at the Israeli embassy tonight," said Hooper.

"Oh....not another reception," sighed Sylvia. "Do we really have to?"

"I know they're tiresome, but Israel is an important ally and it's crucial to keep that Jewish vote happy."

"I suppose....if it's really necessary. But these receptions seem endless."

"That's political life my dear. What we signed on for."

"You mean what you signed on for. I'm just along for the ride."

"Ah, but you're such a dutiful wife. I'm a lucky guy." Hooper smiled at his wife and kissed her gently on the cheek.

"You better believe it, bub. You may be Prime Minister but you better remember who the real boss in this house is."

"Yes, Maam!"

At that moment, Trent Frayne, one of the PM's RCMP security guards popped into the dining room.

"Just checking...everything OK?" he asked.

"We're just fine, Trent," replied Hooper. "Just having some KD with the kids. Would you like some?"

"Er, no sir. Think I'll pass. Enjoy your lunch though. I'll be in the living room if you need anything." Frayne left the room.

* * *

Outside at the front entrance to 24 Sussex Drive, a blue Ford Escape pulled up and parked at the curb.

The five occupants immediately exited the vehicle carrying their weapons. They approached the black iron gate and opened it. Just as they started to enter an RCMP security guard in ceremonial red serge uniform approached.

"Hold on there folks, this is restricted private...." The Mountie suddenly noticed their weapons and reached for his pistol.

Hashim Hadi raised his Uzi. He fired a short burst that stitched the Mountie across the front of his serge jacket. The guard fell to the ground. The five men quickly stepped over the body and made their way to the nearby security guardhouse.

As the terrorists entered, they spotted three policemen inside. One was seated at a computer on a desk, one sitting in a chair reading the Toronto Daily Express, the third talking on the phone.

Before they could make a move, the five men raised their weapons and sprayed the room. It rained blood, flesh, and gray matter as two of the RCMP security men were thrown aside like dolls.

"Red Alert....we have an incursion....," said the police officer on the phone. He just happened to be talking to someone at RCMP headquarters. But he was cut short as a stream of bullets gutted him like a fish.

Silence. The room was now silent with three dead bodies splayed across the furniture.

"Quickly, we must move! They have sounded an alarm," shouted Hadi.

The five men left the building and headed for the front door of the house. As they neared the steps and the black iron railing leading to the green front door, another plain clothes security guard rounded the corner of the house. He had obviously been patrolling the grounds, perhaps he heard the gunfire and came to check it out.

Khaled Kaim raised his AKSU assault rifle. He squeezed off a double-tap that drilled six rounds through the man's chest, puncturing a lung and his aorta.

The Mountie had been reaching for his gun when he staggered to his knees and toppled to the ground. He twitched several times as he profusely bled out.

***

The verbal alarm sounded when the terrorists broke into the guardhouse, immediately prompting a response at RCMP Headquarters. A force of several armed Mounties was immediately dispatched to the PM's residence, the Ottawa Police SWAT team was alerted, as was CSIS.

"My God, this is it!" said CSIS Director Alexander Cuddy when he received word of the attack on the Prime Minister's official residence. "This must be Operation Saladin and the bastards are striking. We need to get over to 24 Sussex right away.

"But sir, is it wise? Perhaps we should leave it to the police," said his deputy director Simon Ward with a nervous twitch. "After all, you're no longer a field officer."

"My God man, we've got terrorists attacking this country and the Prime Minister and his family and you expect me to just sit it out. Not on your goddamn life, Simon. Grab your jacket! You're coming with me. We need to be at the scene."

"Yes, sir," muttered Ward meekly. He followed Cuddy out the door.

***

Trent Frayne heard the gunfire outside and went to the front window to check. What he saw horrified him.

THE SCORPION

There were five armed men heading for the front door. The bloodied body of a security guard lay on the pavement near one of the decorative flower beds.

Instinct kicked in. His job was to protect the PM and his family and it was now one against five. Not good odds.

Frayne burst back into the kitchen.

"Prime Minister, the house is under attack. All of you come with me right now!" barked Frayne.

Hooper seemed surprised, while his wife was shocked and immediately grabbed her two children. The four of them followed Frayne into the living room and headed for the library, a room with the sturdiest wooden oak doors in the house.

As part of the security upgrades to 24 Sussex Drive, there had been talk of building a Panic Room, in case of this very eventuality. But no action had been taken on it yet. The wheels of government run slowly. The library would have to do.

As they neared its entrance, the five men broke through the front doors and Frayne pulled out his Beretta and fired a 9 MM slug at the terrorists. The bullet struck Khaled Kaim in the upper chest. It deflected off a rib bone and exited out of the side of the chest, creating a grisly injury. The terrorist fell. One down.

Frayne moved into the library with the PM's family just as Hadi triggered a short burst from his Uzi. But the bullets struck harmlessly into the wall.

Frayne slammed the huge oak doors shut and locked the door. He moved over to grab a nearby wooden chair and jammed it under the doorknob as extra support.

He pulled out his cell phone and immediately called for backup. Frayne was informed that help was on the way. It would be there in a few minutes.

He only hoped that the door would hold long enough to keep the terrorists out until help arrived. His Beretta was no match for the firepower these intruders carried.

The Prime Minister sat in the room with his family close by. He knew the risks of his job. But felt it unfair that his family was in peril. Sylvia Hooper hugged her children tightly, the terror showing on her frightened face.

They could hear the curses in Arabic outside the room and a banging on the door. The terrorists were apparently trying to ram it with something. But the door was solid oak and wasn't budging.

The four remaining terrorists held a large table they were using to ram the door. They had sprayed it with gun fire but the bullets just chipped the wood off the surface.

As they prepared to take another run at the door, nine figures garbed in black body armor and wearing visors broke into the room. They were members of the

THE SCORPION

Ottawa Police special operations tactical SWAT team and RCMP tactical unit.

"POLICE! DROP YOUR WEAPONS NOW!"

The terrorists ignored the command and turned, ready to fight it out.

A barrage of gunfire erupted in the room. Aaak! Aaak! Aaak! Aaak! The sound of gunfire was deafening. A hail of bullets from automatic weapons sprayed across the room towards the terrorists and a return stream came back at the police, several hitting them in their bulletproof body armor.

"ALLAH AKBAR!" screamed Hadi as he sent a hail of lead at the police SWAT team. Through the corner of his eye, he witnessed Shareet Halaim and Mohammad Amanijad fall amid the shower of bullets. Half of Halaim's head was blown apart, brains and blood spattering behind him and Amanijad took several rounds to the body, stitching its way from his abdomen to his shoulder.

Hadi and Ibrahim Hafiz were all that were left of the terrorist group. They stood their ground and defiantly fired back. Hadi aimed high and took out one of the police officers with a shot through his forehead. *One less infidel!*

But the police firepower was simply too intense. Moments later Hafiz dropped to the ground, his weapon slithering along the carpeted floor.

Only their leader Hadi remained. Determined. Grim. Gritting his teeth. He unleashed another burst of fire before a stream of bullets caught him in the throat. He choked on the blood. His eyes became glassy. Hadi knew he was headed to

Paradise. He smiled as he slid down to the carpet.

Suddenly there was complete silence. It was over.

"CLEAR!" shouted one of the SWAT officers. He walked over to the library door. He knocked loudly and shouted that all was safe.

The door slowly opened and Trent Frayne stood with his Beretta in hand as he checked the scene.

"Is the PM okay?" asked the SWAT officer.

"Everyone's fine," replied Frayne. "Thank God you got here in time. Are they all dead?"

"I don't think there's any doubt about that. We'll call the meat wagon."

As the men checked the five bodies and tended to their fallen officer, although he was beyond help, several more people entered the house through the front door.

One was RCMP Commissioner Brent Haycroft accompanied by CSIS Director Alexander Cuddy and his deputy Simon Ward.

Cuddy was horrified at the scene and the carnage that had been unleashed. Prime Minister Hooper emerged from the library after telling his wife and kids to stay put. He didn't want to subject them to the images in the living room.

Cuddy hurried over to the PM. "Prime Minister, so glad you and your family are safe. We had word of a terrorist attack but never expected anything like this."

"We're fine, Alex. Thanks to the fine work of the Ottawa PD and RCMP. I guess these guys didn't vote for me." Hooper still had his sense of humor.

"I'm so sorry, sir that we weren't able to stop them before it got this far," said Cuddy. "We knew they were in the country but they dropped out of sight. We never knew their target."

"Don't worry about it, Alex. All's well that ends well. You did your best I'm sure."

Cuddy nodded grimly. "Well, at least it's a relief to know that Operation Saladin failed. We can all breathe a lot easier now that we know it's over."

Cuddy wondered which of the fallen terrorists was The Scorpion.

CHAPTER 45

ST. MATTHEW'S UNITED CHURCH, TORONTO

THE WEDDING PARTY gathered inside the church. There was a buzz of excitement and anticipation.

Katie Cannon and Andrew Chase stood before the Minister, Rev. Terry O'Connell as he explained the procedures they would follow at tomorrow's ceremony. They practised their vows and the exchange of rings as Maid of Honor Donna Marie Pierce and Best Man Paul Mann stood by.

Katie had opted for two other bridesmaids, Karmen Delaney and Judy North close friends from her university days. They stood by all dressed casually in jeans and sweatshirts for the rehearsal.

Katie's Mom and Dad, Norma and Herbert Cannon were seated in the pews along with Braden Young and Leah McCall who had been invited to attend the rehearsal and the dinner reception afterwards.

After they finished their vows, Andrew planted his lips on Katie.

"That's really not necessary tonight," said Rev. O'Connell with a smile.

"Oh, it most definitely is," quipped Andrew. "Practice makes perfect."

"Now Andrew, behave yourself," said Katie. "Getting nervous? Only a few hours left as a bachelor. And I won't be sharing you after we're married."

"I can hardly wait. How about you?"

"A tad nervous. But not about getting married. I'm just afraid I'll do something to screw up the ceremony."

Andrew reached out and gently pulled her close to him. "You'll be fine, sweetie. You just need to show up and look beautiful. It's going to be a wedding that we will both remember all our lives."

Katie dearly hoped that was true.

CHAPTER 46
ROYAL YORK HOTEL

THE SCORPION and Ali Saleh sat in their hotel room watching the grim news on television.

A reporter stood outside the Prime Minister's residence recounting details of the thwarted attack by terrorists on 24 Sussex Drive. The reporter interviewed police and CSIS officials about the incident.

"Through a combined operation with the RCMP and Ottawa Police Department we fortunately were able to stop this assassination attempt on our Prime Minister," said a sombre Alexander Cuddy speaking to the cameras. "The five terrorists were killed and we are confident that no further threat to the security of the nation remains."

The Scorpion switched off the TV.

He remained calm although he was deeply disappointed that this phase of the operation had failed. On the plus side, it gained significant media attention for their cause. The sacrifice of the five brothers was not in vain.

"Don't worry, Ali," said the Scorpion. "Tomorrow's operation will be an even bigger blow to the infidels. They won't know what hit them."

THE SCORPION

JAMES A. ANDERSON

DAY SEVEN

SATURDAY

CHAPTER 47

ST. MATTHEW'S UNITED CHURCH

IT WAS a grand day for a wedding. The sun shone brightly amid clear blue skies as guests filtered up the steps into the church.

Andrew Chase stood at the entrance with Paul Mann greeting guests and nervously chatting. He glanced at his Rolex. 10:46 a.m. The ceremony was scheduled to start at 11 a.m., but the bride had yet to arrive.

Rev. Terry O'Connell walked over to Andrew."It's getting near time. Perhaps we should go into the church before Katie arrives."

"Certainly, Reverend. Lead on. I'm completely in your hands."

They entered the church and made their way down the aisle to the front altar.

The church pews were filled with people as the organist played Handel's *Water Music*.

It seemed an eternity before the Minister suddenly stood to attention and quietly gave the signal to Andrew and Paul. The organist started belting out Wagner's *Bridal Chorus* from *Lohengrin*, the traditional wedding march.

Andrew turned and saw a breathtaking sight.

Donna Marie Pierce led the bridesmaids, wearing dark, purple dresses, up the aisle. They were followed by Katie on the arm of her father, Herbert. She appeared absolutely stunning in her virginal white Vera Wang wedding gown. She looked and felt like a princess.

As the party reached the front of the church, Herbert handed her off to Andrew whispering, "Take good care of her my boy."

"I will," Andrew whispered back.

"Dearly beloved, we are gathered here today to join in holy matrimony Andrew James Chase and Katie Pearl Cannon....." began Rev. O'Connell.

The ceremony went off beautifully for about 15 minutes when Katie and Andrew said their final vows to each other. They were pronounced husband and wife. The kiss they shared was as light as rose petals.

Andrew looked Katie in the eyes and said, "Oh, my sweet love. I've been waiting my whole life for you."

"Me too," replied Katie.

CHAPTER 48

CHAUCER'S BAR & GRILL

WHILE THE WEDDING party was off getting the official photos taken at the Toronto botanical gardens, Braden Young, Leah McCall, Trevor Trevanian and Lynne Whitfield killed time having lunch and some drinks at this nearby restaurant. They had a few hours until the reception and dinner at the CN Tower that evening.

"So Trev, how's the book coming?" asked Young.

"Nearly done. Down to the final chapters," replied Trevanian. "Then I have some revisions and editing to do before turning it into the publisher. It's due by August."

"Well, I'm sure it'll be a huge hit. Now that bin Laden is gone, you were probably one of the last people to talk to him before the Americans finally nailed his ass. Can't say that he will be missed terribly."

"Anyway, I owe a lot to you Braden for getting me out of that jam in Pakistan. How on earth did you spring me from Pakistani Intelligence anyway? That would be useful info for my book."

"I called in a huge favour from the big guy in the White House who called the Pakistani President personally. We needed that interview as soon as possible."

"Well, again my thanks. You really saved my ass on that one."

Braden turned his attention to Lynne. "So Lynne, how long have you two been an item?"

"Not long," said Lynne. "We just met earlier this week. How about you and Leah?"

"Oh, we've been together about seven months. But she's the best thing that's happened to me in some time."

Lynne smiled. "That's nice. Maybe yours will be the next wedding we get to attend."

"Don't know about that," Braden replied as he moved to grasp Leah's hand. "We don't want to jinx things. My first wedding didn't end too well. We're just enjoying each other's company and we'll see where it takes us."

Trevor, sipping his Rickards Red, decided to change the topic away from weddings. "Say Braden, what about that news last night about the terrorist attack on the Prime Minister? Talk about brazen. Was it Al-Qaeda?"

"They think so. We have the story in today's paper from Dave Mariash, our bureau man in Ottawa. "Something about an Operation Saladin. The intelligence boys got advance word that something was up but they weren't able to find these bastards until they struck. They're all dead though, so that should be an end to it.

Thank God, the PM is safe. Can you believe it? They actually found a scimitar with one of these fuckers and the police think they planned to behead Hooper."

"Maybe you could find out more information about this operation through your contacts, hon," piped up Lynne.

"No. I don't have anything to do with Al-Qaida any more and that suits me just fine," said Trevor. "I only hope it truly is the end of it and they don't have anything else planned over here."

CHAPTER 49

ROYAL YORK HOTEL

THE SCORPION picked up the suitcase nuke and placed it on the bed. He beckoned Ali Saleh to come over so he could explain how to operate the device.

It was very compact, designed to be portable. Al-Qaeda had obtained it from a Russian arms dealer. This particular device was a small 1-kiloton bomb. The warhead of a suitcase nuke consists of a tube with two pieces of uranium which when rammed together would trigger a blast. The case contained a high explosive detonator, a battery and an arming switch.

The Scorpion demonstrated to Saleh how to arm the device and showed him the trigger switch to set off the explosion. He planned to be miles away at the airport when the bomb went off.

People in the immediate vicinity of the detonation would die from the force of the explosion itself and likely be vaporized. The blast radius would be about 1.5 miles because of the altitude of the detonation. The big killer would be the radiation that would spread over miles, causing radiation poisoning and sickness. Over time, exposed people in the affected area also would be subject to risks of cancer.

THE SCORPION

Just the thought of it brought joy to the Scorpion's heart. The infidels would experience death and destruction on a scale they could never imagine. It would strike fear into them and into the Great Satan to the south.

As he reflected on his teenage boyhood in Iraq, images came back to the Scorpion of his dead mother, father and sister from American Smart bombs that levelled their residential home in Baghdad. He had been away from home at the time or else he would have been among the mangled bodies.

But he had been spared and he vowed to bring revenge on the Americans and their allies who had unleashed such a firestorm of death and destruction. Shock and Awe they called it. Collateral damage.

Well, now we will bring a firestorm to them in their own backyard, the Scorpion thought. *I'll show them shock and awe!*

CHAPTER 50

360 RESTAURANT, CN TOWER

IT WAS ALMOST 5:30 p.m. and guests started arriving at the CN Tower restaurant for the Chase wedding reception at 6 p.m. Dinner would follow at 7.

Restaurant staff were scurrying about, busy finalizing arrangements at the more than 75 tables in the room. Guests began to congregate in a bar area at the side, talking and sipping on their beverages.

Braden Young and Leah McCall stood with their drinks in hand chatting with Trevor Trevanian and Lynne Whitfield. They had checked the seating chart and found they were seated together at Table 4, right near the front head table. Close to all the wedding action.

Braden peered around the room and saw many prominent faces from the community. Over in one corner of the room, he saw the Mayor of Toronto, the Chief of Police, The Fire Chief, several prominent members of provincial and federal parliaments, including some cabinet ministers. A high-powered guest list indeed.

Braden couldn't help but think of the damage that a bomb in this room

THE SCORPION

would inflict. But he immediately dismissed the thought as nonsense.

* * *

The Scorpion and his sidekick Ali Saleh had made their way to the CN Tower and up to the restaurant level on the upper deck. The Scorpion was carrying the briefcase. They passed through guests into the kitchen and the back service areas. They found an isolated area. Now they just needed to wait.

Fifteen minutes later, a waiter wearing a white jacket and black trousers passed by them. The Scorpion saw the area was clear. He moved quickly. He grabbed the man around the neck. A thin wire was in his hand. He looped it around the waiter's neck and pulled tightly. He garrotted him quietly and efficiently.

He and Saleh dragged the body into a nearby empty anteroom. The Scorpion stripped the body of the uniform which he handed to Saleh and told him to put it on.

"Now we just need another one," said the Scorpion. "You wait here."

He left the room.

About 20 minutes later he came back with another body. Within minutes the Scorpion was attired in the waiter's uniform. The two bodies were left sprawled in a corner in only their underwear. The Scorpion opened a cupboard and gently stored the briefcase inside. Until it was time.

The two terrorists then went to the kitchen to mingle with the chefs busily preparing the meals and the other servers who were scurrying about with trays of drinks and hors d'oeuvres.

"You two," barked a voice from a bulky man who was obviously a supervisor. "Take some drink trays out to the guests."

"Yes, sir," replied the Scorpion humbly. He and Saleh picked up two trays filled with glasses of champagne and circulated among the guests.

Things were going exactly according to plan.

THE SCORPION

CHAPTER 51

360 RESTAURANT, CN TOWER

DINNER HAD BEEN SERVED. The servers were busy gathering up dishes and started to put out the dessert – key lime pie. They were also offering the guests coffee and tea.

The formal ceremonies would be starting soon, but Trevor was having trouble concentrating. Lynne had been fondling him underneath the table and he was heavily aroused. *Naughty girl!* Trevor felt like he was living that scene from the 1989 movie *When Harry Met Sally* in which Meg Ryan was having an orgasm in the restaurant, only in reverse.

"Stop it," whispered Trevor.

"Can't help it, I'm horny," grinned Lynne. "Let's go somewhere more private.

"What, now? You've got to be kidding. The speeches will be starting soon."

"What would you rather have, darling, some boring speeches or me?"

Trevor put down his napkin and made an excuse for them to leave.

They quickly made their way out of the room and down a corridor.

* * *

Best Man Paul Mann stood at the microphone at the head table podium giving his speech. He recalled some of the antics Andrew and he got up to at university. Paul spoke for several minutes, generating plenty of laughs from the audience. As he began to introduce the Maid of Honor Donna Marie Pierce to speak next, people tinkled their glasses – a signal for the bride and groom to kiss. Andrew and Katie obliged to loud applause.

The ceremonies continued. Everyone was having a wonderful time.

* * *

So were Trevor and Lynne who couldn't keep their hands off each other. Trevor pushed a nearby room door and they entered. Lynne kissed him passionately as they entered the room and moved toward a nearby couch in the room.

Suddenly Trevor felt Lynne's body freeze. She was rigid.

"What's the matter, hon?" he asked perplexed.

"Look! There!" She pointed to the corner of the room.

Trevor gazed in that direction and saw the two near naked bodies sprawled in a heap.

"MY GOD!"

Trevor and Lynne walked over to the bodies and Trevor checked for life signs. "They're both dead! And from the ligature marks on their necks it appears they were both garrotted. What the hell's going on here? Who commits murder at a

THE SCORPION

bloody wedding and why?"

"Who are they?" asked Lynne.

"I have no idea. But they may have been restaurant servers and someone's obviously taken their uniforms and their place. Something's rotten here. Somebody's up to no good and people at this wedding may be in danger. We need to alert the police."

Just as they prepared to leave the room, two waiters entered. When they saw the two people in the room, they both drew guns.

The Scorpion and Ali Saleh waved Beretta 93-Rs at Trevor and Lynne.

"Who are you?" asked the Scorpion. "And why are you in this room?"

"I might ask you the same question. And why are you pointing guns at us? Is this standard hardware for restaurant servers these days?" replied Trevor.

"Shut up, infidel!" barked Saleh. "We must shoot them."

"No, Ali" said the Scorpion. "The sound will draw too much attention. We can't afford to have people come to investigate. We must act now before it is too late. Our plans must change. It appears I will be joining you in Paradise this day after all."

The Scorpion ordered Trevor and Lynne to move back and sit on the couch. "Get the briefcase, Ali."

Ali Saleh padded over to the cupboard and retrieved the briefcase.

He opened it and stood awaiting further instructions.

The Scorpion smiled. "My friends, this is a compact nuclear device, which in a few minutes will be blowing us all to Kingdom come."

"Listen, you don't have to do this. I'm a reporter," said Trevor. "If you have grievances, I can do a story that airs them to the public."

"Nothing you can write can resolve our grievances with your heathen society and your American allies," sneered the Scorpion. "Ali, arm the device and prepare to detonate. The Scorpion meanwhile had walked closer to the couch.

Trevor felt the blood rushing to his ears. He flexed his knees and launched himself off the couch. He gave the Scorpion a kick in the chest that sent him flying to the corner. His Baretta skidded along the floor away from him

"Don't do anything stupid. Stay where you are," Trevor shouted at the Scorpion, his voice trembling slightly. But the scorpion made a dash at him. He grabbed Trevor and struck him sharply in the jaw with his fist. Trevor fell back.

"Put the briefcase down immediately!" shouted Lynne at Saleh. She was pointing her Walther PPK at him. She had retrieved it from the holster strapped to her thigh. Lynne never went anywhere without her gun nearby, even to a wedding. You just never knew when you were going to need it.

Salah just grinned. "ALLAH AKBAR!!" He moved his finger toward the detonation switch.

THE SCORPION

Lynne fired. An expression of surprise showed on Saleh's face. A dark hole appeared in his forehead dead centre between his eyes, blood seeping out of it. The briefcase slipped from his fingers to the floor and he slumped down.

Lynne immediately swung the gun over to the Scorpion.

But no one was there.

CHAPTER 52

CN TOWER

POLICE, EMT and Hazmat officials swarmed all over the anteroom. CSIs were gathering forensic evidence from the shooting. Saleh's body still lay on the floor.

Trevor and Lynne watched as a Hazmat officer took the deadly briefcase from the room, presumably to a location where it could safely be disarmed.

They were extensively interviewed by police detective Peter Moon and outlined the details of what transpired. They told Moon of the other terrorist who disappeared and the police issued an APB based on their description of the man.

Lynne also finally revealed to the police and Trevor that she was an MI-6 agent investigating terrorist links.

"Thank God you happened on the scene when you did," said Moon. "Otherwise Katie's wedding would have been spoiled." He had an ironic smile.

"That's an understatement to say the least," said Trevor.

Moon turned serious again. "No, this city owes you both a lot. You prevented a major catastrophe here today. One that no one knew was coming."

"Well, I guess it's one way to get an exclusive story," remarked Trevor. " I know what will be making the front page of the Daily Express tomorrow and

Braden doesn't even know about it yet."

After they finished with Moon, Lynne and Trevor walked out of the room and back toward the restaurant area where the wedding reception was still going full blast, the participants still blithely unaware of the drama that had occurred only a few feet away.

As they peered into the room, they heard the DJ's music belting out and Anne Murray singing "Nobody Loves Me Like You Do". Katie and Andrew were having the bride and groom's first dance.

"Shall we tell them?" asked Lynne.

"No. Let them enjoy themselves. They'll all find out soon enough. Speaking of telling the truth, were you ever going to tell me you were MI-6? Was I just an assignment to you?"

"It started out that way, Trevor. My bosses were convinced you had Al-Qaeda contacts deep inside the organization and wanted me to shadow you to try and find out who they were. But I really liked you and developed feelings for you. I didn't like what I was doing and it became clear you're not in league with Al-Qaeda."

"You've got that right. That whole thing with bin Laden was a fluke. A lucky one mind you as it turned out. They kidnapped me in Afghanistan and I had no idea where they were taking me. I thought I was going to be killed or held for ransom."

"I came to realize that," said Lynne. "And that's what I told them when I refused to carry on with the assignment yesterday. They weren't very happy when I told them. I don't know if I'll even have a job when I get back to London."

"Oh, don't worry about that, hon. By the time I'm finished writing the story – you're going to be the hero who singlehandedly saved the City of Toronto from a nuclear holocaust."

"Makes you wonder what would have happened if I hadn't gotten so horny, doesn't it?" Lynne smiled with a mischievous glint in her eye.

"I think that part, we'd better leave out of the story," stated Trevor.

EPILOGUE
A 747 OVER THE ATLANTIC

THE MAN in seat 7A relaxed and sat back to enjoy the flight. It would be several hours until he arrived in Frankfurt. He planned to catch some sleep. It had been a trying day.

The Scorpion felt uneasy. His mission was a failure. This was the first time he had ever failed. He felt humiliated and angry.

Still, he tried to look on the positive side. He had escaped. He was still alive rather than being atomized in a nuclear blast. He lived to fight another day and to bring retribution to the infidels.

And upon reflection he realized the mission had not been a total failure. The assaults on the Prime Minister and the CN Tower were a huge lesson to the infidel devils.

They were never safe. The arm of Al-Qaeda was capable of reaching them anywhere and anytime.

Yes, things are not so bleak after all. I will return.

The End.....Or is it?

ABOUT THE AUTHOR

James A. Anderson is a retired journalist and graduate of McMaster University in Hamilton, Ontario. He lives in London, Ontario, Canada with his wife Sherry and two basenjis, Remba and Wakili. They have two married children, Mike and Amanda and four grandchildren, Katie, Trevor, Megan and Leah.

James A. Anderson is also the author of the best selling thriller DEADLINE (2010).

What readers are saying about DEADLINE

"A remarkable debut. . .A real page-turner." – Joan Hall Hovey, Author of *Night Corridor*

'Non-stop action and thrill a minute." Arthur J. Levine, Author of *Johnny Oops* and *Johnny Oops II –Timeless*

"Stark, vivid, black and white newspaper thriller. Really excellent. Very engaging....." – Barry Eysman, Author of *Dancers in the Sky*

"This author skillfully combines several sub-plots, weaving them together to paint a picture of the hectic, crime-filled life of the staff on a major daily newspaper. Alternating chapters keep one turning the pages, eager to find out what happens next to the key characters. . ." – Sarah A. Blane, Author of *The Widow's Revenge*

"Loved this book, full of intrigue and twists and turns. . . Hold on to your seats for the ride of a lifetime." Mel Comley, Author of the D.I. Lorne Simpkins series

"DEADLINE reminded me of one of those old black and white movies with the newspaper reporters scrambling to stay on top of the story. It had a vintage sort of feel. . . Overall the story moved along at a good pace and tension was high." Barbara Ellen Brink, Author of *Crushed* and *Entangled*

JAMES A. ANDERSON

"DEADLINE is a tightly woven novel about the guts of a Daily newspaper in a major metropolitan city. . . The timeline in DEADLINE will keep you turning the pages breathlessly!" J. D. Michael Phelps, Author of *Execution of Justice*

"Great New Talent - An Assured Debut..." – Barry Crowther, Author of *Missing (The Matt Spears Mysteries)*

"This is a gripping tale that you will have to finish before you put it to bed!" – Susan J. McArthur, Author of *Soul and Shadow*

"DEADLINE is a fast-paced, multi-faceted, and suspenseful read." –Rebecca Stroud, Author of *Devil's Moon*

THE SCORPION

An Excerpt from DEADLINE

Chapter 1

Toronto   Wednesday   11:25 PM (EDT)

HIS TARGET came into view.

She strolled casually down the concrete steps of the 18-storey office tower located downtown on Bay Street.

It was a muggy night. The humid weather was typical for mid-August. The temperature sign on a nearby building flashed 25 Celsius, but it felt more like 30 degrees. The air felt hot and steamy, conditions that caused clothing to cling tightly to the body. It felt like walking fully clothed into a steam bath.

His eyes followed her as she casually walked on the pavement. Her lithe body was elegantly attired in a trim, form-fitting grey skirt and matching jacket. Her short-length honey blond hair slightly swaying with the movement. She carried an attaché case, very businesslike. Her high heels ticktocked a steady rhythm on the sidewalk.

His excitement began to build.

Antoinette Bower was an up and coming young lawyer. Her night work with Bannerman, Evers, Ingham and Otis was typical for her heavy caseload. Many nights Bower worked until after midnight.

Today was slightly easier as she completed preparations for her court date tomorrow morning at 9 a.m. Time to walk home to her apartment eight blocks away.

She looked forward to a nice hot soak with bubble bath, a martini and an hour or so with a good trashy romance novel. It was the only romance in her life right now.

At age 28, Bower was too busy building a legal career to get seriously involved with men.

Yes, that sounded made to order for her tonight. Bower's thoughts were so concentrated on getting home she failed to notice the street was strangely deserted at this hour. There were no other pedestrians around and only the odd passing vehicle.

Bower also didn't observe the maroon Ford Explorer pulling up slowly behind her. He drove slowly, closely scanning the street ahead and beside him. The moonlit street was isolated except for the occasional passing vehicle. He saw her turn down a side street just a few yards ahead.

Perfect.

THE SCORPION

Bower moved down the side street. The entrance to her apartment building was only a few hundred yards ahead. Home Sweet Home came to mind. Her thoughts were suddenly interrupted.

"Excuse me, Miss," said a bewildered voice. "I'm new to the city and I'm trying to find a friend on Lombard Street. Is it anywhere near here?"

Bower now saw the Explorer parked alongside her at the curb. A man behind the wheel was leaning over and speaking through the open passenger side window.

A sense of apprehension and caution immediately overcame her. She realized she was alone on the street with a male stranger in a parked vehicle. All the signs screamed she should ignore the man's request and walk away.

"Listen, I realize this must be distressing to you at this time of night. I assure you I'm harmless. I'm just a guy who is lost late at night. I have a map here but it is hard to make out where exactly I am in relation to Lombard Street. Any help would be most appreciated."

"Okay, but I'd like you to get out of the car and bring the map here." Bower cautiously kept her distance from the vehicle.

The man stepped out from the Explorer with a map in hand. He stood next to Antoinette Bower holding the map as she tried to explain directions to Lombard Street.

"It's only a few blocks this way," she pointed to the map. "You're not far wrong."

His other hand emerged from a side pocket. A handkerchief edged upward as the stranger let the map drop to the ground. Bower suddenly felt a vice-like grip.

She started to struggle. A scream began to surface, but was suddenly cut off. The handkerchief smothered her mouth. She sensed the strong smell of a chemical odour. She briefly continued to struggle but an overwhelming drowsiness arose.

Then everything went black.

The Wolfman had his next victim.

DEADLINE is available in ebook and paperback from Amazon.com, Barnes and Noble.com, Smashwords.com and Lulu.com

Made in the USA
Charleston, SC
21 April 2012